COURAGEOUS
BRIDE

By Jane Peart

The Brides of Montclair Series

Valiant Bride
Ransomed Bride
Fortune's Bride
Folly's Bride
Yankee Bride/Rebel Bride
Gallant Bride
Shadow Bride
Destiny's Bride
Jubilee Bride
Mirror Bride
Hero's Bride
Senator's Bride
Daring Bride
Courageous Bride

The Westward Dreams Series

Runaway Heart
Promise of the Valley
Where Tomorrow Waits
A Distant Dawn

The American Quilt Series

The Pattern
The Pledge
The Promise

COURAGEOUS BRIDE

MONTCLAIR
in WARTIME
1939–1946

By *best-selling author*

JANE PEART

ZondervanPublishingHouse
Grand Rapids, Michigan

A Division of HarperCollins*Publishers*

Courageous Bride
Copyright © 1998 by Jane Peart

Requests for information should be addressed to:

📘 ZondervanPublishingHouse
Grand Rapids, Michigan 49530

Library of Congress Cataloging-in-Publication Data

Peart, Jane.
    Courageous bride : Montclair in wartime, 1939–1946 / Jane Peart.
       p. cm. — (The brides of Montclair series : 14)
       ISBN: 0-310-20210-8
    1. World War, 1939–1945—Fiction. I. Title. II. Series: Peart, Jane. Brides of
Montclair series : bk. 14.
PS3566.E238C68 1998
813'.54—dc21   98-5496
                                        CIP

Printed in the United States of America

---

98 99 00 01 02 03 04 /❖ DC/ 10 9 8 7 6 5 4 3

1939

chapter

1

Montclair
Spring 1939

CARA MONTROSE, A TALL, slender woman in her early forties, wearing a threadbare riding jacket, tan breeches, and scuffed leather boots, came out of the house and walked purposefully toward the stables. Her dark auburn hair was pulled back into a clubbed knot at the nape of her neck. Today her face, with its aristocratic features, was unusually thoughtful, almost pensive.

She moved with a casual grace along a path bordered with golden daffodils. As if becoming suddenly aware of them, she paused briefly, bent to touch a delicate, bonnet-shaped flower with one finger. Straightening, she breathed deeply of the scent of apple blossoms wafting from the orchard.

Virginia in early spring was truly paradise. No wonder she had never been really happy anywhere but here. She looked back at the house where she had come as a bride over ten years ago. Seen through a veil of pink-and-white dogwood, it stood as it had for nearly two hundred years, its mellowed brick chimneys rising over the rambling slate roof. Montclair. It had become almost as dear to her as Cameron Hall, where she had grown up.

If only she and Kip could keep it up the way it should be. But help being what it was these days, and money in the Montrose bank account being what it usually was, there was no possibility of that. At least not right away. Someday . . . perhaps.

In the meantime she had her pony class to teach three days a week, and that brought in a little income. Kip's small income as an army reserve flight instructor helped, as did the income from the occasional chartered flights he piloted.

For a short period he had flown for the airmail service. But unpredictable weather often grounded him for days as he waited for clearance to take off. It also meant being away from home too much, and Kip loved his family and missed them terribly when he was gone. Now his main job was giving flying lessons to a few adventurous souls at the local airfield.

We're doing the best we can, Cara thought, her jaw tightening as she recalled how Great Aunt Garnet had chastised her for advertising her pony classes. "Don't you care what people say?" the old lady had demanded.

"No, I don't care what people say," Cara had replied. "I never have and I don't intend to start now." So what if people thought they were broke? So were most of the families they knew. There was a depression on in the country.

Thank goodness they had managed to scrape enough together and get a bank loan so Luc could attend the university. Smart boy that he was, Luc had also earned a scholarship. She didn't know what they'd do about Niki when her turn came.

The five ponies were kept in the small barn next to the stables. Cara went to each one, fed them sugar cubes from the supply she carried in her jacket pocket. She rubbed their noses and talked to them softly, gently. Like children, the ponies were much more tractable when they were sweet-talked, not scolded. Amused at her own analogy, Cara got down the tack and started getting the animals ready for their little riders, who were due within the next half hour.

Cara was tightening the girth strap on one of the ponies when she heard the sound of voices. She turned to see the girl and boy approaching. They did not see her as they went inside the stable. Niki's voice was raised argumentatively. She was probably trying to get Luc's opinion, advice, or approval. He seemed to be listening intently to whatever it was she was saying. Still not aware of Cara's presence, they got their horses out of their stalls and began to saddle them. Cara stood at the entrance of the pony barn, watching them fondly.

Luc was becoming an extraordinarily handsome young man. Although not as tall as his father, he had a slim, athletic build and Kip's coloring and features. Corduroy breeches, a blue denim shirt with the sleeves rolled up, and a red scarf tied casually around his neck gave him a dashing look.

Of course, Niki was as carelessly outfitted as ever, in a sweater yards too big for her, jodhpurs too short, her curly dark hair as tousled as some ragamuffin boy's. She was still talking as she swung up into her saddle. Luc mounted with effortless grace, and they walked their horses out of the barn and into the sunlit afternoon.

"Have a good ride," Cara called. Neither seemed to have heard her over the clatter of their horses' hooves on the cobblestone. At the curve of the drive they broke into a trot. Cara remained, looking after them until they rode out of sight.

From the day Cara and Kip had brought the little French war-orphan back to Montclair, Luc, although only two years older, had taken on the role of a protective older brother, affectionate and kind. Niki adored him immediately, wanting to tag along with him everywhere. Tolerantly Luc put up with her.

However, how long would this close relationship last? Home from his first year at college, Luc was changing, growing up to be a serious, more thoughtful young man. Cara had found books on his bedside table, placed facedown as if he had been reading at night before turning out the light. This was a new side of Luc, one she had not been aware of before. Certainly this wasn't the Kip part of Luc. Cara couldn't remember the last time she had seen Kip reading a book. If ever. Maybe he'd occasionally pick up a *Field and Stream* magazine or glance through the Hunt Club newsletter . . .

"Afternoon, Aunt Cara." The young male voice startled her, and she whirled around to see her nephew Stewart Cameron.

"Well, hello, Stew," she greeted him, thinking the lanky redhead was, as they say, the "spittin' image" of her brother Scott at the same age. "Shouldn't you be working at the newspaper this time of day? Does your daddy, the editor, know you're playing hooky?"

"Turned in my copy. Got a city council meeting to cover tonight, so I took the rest of the day off." He grinned, then glanced into the barn hopefully. "Niki around?"

Cara darted him a quick look, then shook her head. "Sorry, she and Luc just took off on a ride."

Stewart could not hide his disappointment. He did not have a poker face, Cara thought with sympathetic amusement. "They should be back in an hour or so, Stew. I told them I wanted them back in plenty of time to clean up and help me some. Your Aunt Kitty and Craig are in Williamsburg, and they're driving over here for supper." Cara added impulsively, "You're welcome to join us, if you'd like."

The minute the words were out of her mouth, Cara winced. *Niki will kill me.* She always wanted Luc to herself when he was home for the weekend. But it was too late to retract the invitation. Stewart's face broke into an eager grin.

"Thanks, I'd like that, if it isn't any trouble."

"No trouble. It will be just family. You're family, Stew."

When Luc and Niki came back and found Stewart there, Cara was relieved to see Niki hide her chagrin. Sometimes Niki treated Stewart with undisguised indifference. Maybe Niki was learning to curb her impulsiveness. Cara hoped so. Niki's volatile temperament had often got her into trouble. Cara set another place at the dining room table, thinking that she couldn't really blame Stewart for having fallen in love with her adopted daughter. Niki had become an enchanting young woman.

She wasn't beautiful, but her face had individuality. Brown eyes sparkling with mischievousness, a small, square-tipped nose, a generous mouth ready to smile. Her silky dark hair was worn short and gave her the look of a French street urchin—which might have been her destiny if Cara had not rescued her from the orphanage and brought her to Virginia after the war.

Upstairs, after a quick shower, Niki fumed. For all her effort to maintain a good-natured acceptance, she *had* been dismayed to find Stewart Cameron waiting when she and Luc cantered into the stable yard. She had hoped that when Aunt Kitty and her husband and Tante and Uncle Kip lingered at the table over coffee, she and Luc could slip away for a private conversation. There was so much she wanted to tell him, confide to him, and she hadn't had a chance on their gallop that afternoon. Whenever Luc came home to Montclair on weekends, he always wanted to ride hard. "Get the cobwebs out," he called it. Niki couldn't imagine why Luc had chosen to work in the stuffy Richmond office of Frank Maynard, their state senator. Now, with Stewart here, there probably wouldn't be another chance. She'd just have to find some time before Luc left on Sunday evening to tell him her plans. He'd probably try to talk her out of them, but maybe not. If anyone would understand, it would be Luc.

Niki felt her unhappiness come down upon her like some nightmarish entity. The dark cloud she mostly kept at bay descended, twisting and turning inside, making everything seem dreary, when in reality everything was lovely.

She lived in a beautiful home, with affectionate people who showered her with everything anyone could want or dream of having. Why was it not enough? Why did she feel claustrophobic?

It wasn't as though she didn't appreciate Tante and all she had done for her. That painful empty place she had in her heart had nothing to do with Tante. It was the not knowing that hurt. Like a toothache that wouldn't go away, would *never* go away until she had a chance to find out—or at least to *try* to find out.

Well, somehow she'd have to get through dinner and hope Stewart would leave early. She gave her hair a couple of whacks with the brush, made a final check in the mirror, and then went downstairs.

After dessert, instead of excusing the young people while the adults stayed at the table, as was their custom, Tante suggested that since the evening was warm, they should have their coffee on the veranda. Picking up the silver coffee carafe, Cara signaled Niki to help her. Resignedly Niki followed with the tray of cups and saucers.

On the porch everyone took seats on the wicker armchairs or in one of the rocking chairs and resumed the conversation. Niki went from one to the other, offering them cream and sugar. Watching her, Kitty Cavanaugh, Cara's twin, thought it was uncanny how alike the two were. Not in appearance but in personality. Kitty had noticed it even when Niki was a little girl. Now it was even more apparent. They both had the same spontaneous gaiety, a longing for attention, an eagerness to please. It was all the more endearing because Niki had a certain unsureness about her, a vulnerability that Cara never had. Cara was always supremely confident of her ability to make people love her. There was something a little hesitant about Niki.

When Niki reached her, Kitty asked, "So Nicole, now that you'll be graduating from high school, what do you plan to do?"

Afterward Niki never knew why she said it. Maybe because it had been on her mind all through dinner as she waited for a chance to talk to Luc about her plan. At Kitty's question she just blurted out, "What I really want to do, Aunt Kitty, is go to France, see if I can find my real parents."

Her answer seemed to drop into a pool of utter stillness. It was one of those silences that sometimes fall naturally, even during the liveliest gatherings. The statement hung there vibrating until someone had the presence of mind to pick up the thread of the previous discussion and carry on with it. Soon the buzz of voices continued.

If her hands had been free, Niki would have clapped one over her mouth. If she hadn't tightly gripped the tray she was holding, she might have dropped it, spilling everything all over Aunt Kitty's lovely dress and making a terrible mess. Instead she'd made a *different* kind of mess.

Automatically both Kitty and Niki glanced at Cara. At the sight of her suddenly pale face, her stunned expression, both realized that she had not only overheard Niki's reply but had been shocked by it. Niki's wide-eyed, stricken gaze met Kitty's.

It was not Cara's nature to show hurt, and she did not do so now under Kitty's sympathetic gaze. Instead she turned to Craig and continued their conversation, which had momentarily halted.

Indeed, Cara had heard every word. Even as she kept her voice calm, she was deeply moved. How long had Niki kept this hidden, harbored a secret plan? She had been just four when Cara and Kip married and brought her back to live at Montclair.

Cara assumed Niki remembered little if anything about the French orphanage where Cara had worked after the war and where Niki had been brought as an abandoned baby. Niki had never before expressed the desire to find her real parents. *Why now?* Cara wondered. *And why does this natural curiosity upset me so much?* Maybe if she and Kip had had other children of their own ... maybe then she could be less wounded by what Niki wanted to do. And what if Niki were somehow able to track down her real parents and they were people whom she couldn't love, admire—or worse still, who did not want her?

As soon as she could, Niki made her escape back to the kitchen, where Luc found her a few minutes later.

"What was all that about?" he demanded.

She whirled around from the sink, where she had been standing, clutching the metal edges of the drainboard, trying to stop shaking. "Well, it's true. It's something I've been thinking about for a long time."

"I don't think you picked the best possible time to announce it," Luc said dryly.

"I didn't intend to. . . . I—"

"Niki, you never *intend* to do some of the dumb things you do, do you? You just act on impulse. Never mind if you upset things that get in your way," he said, half smiling. Both of them remembered some of their early quarrels, when Niki would run into the room so eager to share something with him that she didn't see one of the elaborate Lego structures he used to build, and inadvertently knock it down.

"I guess I could have—"

"Yes, you certainly could have," Luc drawled, then came over and put a comforting arm around her shoulders. "So, want to tell me about it?"

"You of all people, Luc, should understand why it's impor- tant. I know you love Tante and Uncle Kip is your father, but

14

you've had a chance to find out about your real mother and know your grandparents."

Every summer since he was fifteen, Luc had traveled to France to visit his mother's parents, the Boulangers. The first year he went with Jill Cameron, who went to see the one remaining member of her family, an aging uncle in England. From that time on Luc traveled on his own. When he came home each fall, he had many fascinating stories to share. While using his grandparents' home as his base, he had taken bicycle trips all over France with his companion, Paul Duval, who over the years had become Luc's best friend in their village. Paul had even come back with Luc to stay for his junior year in high school at Montclair.

Perhaps these experiences of Luc's had made Niki more aware of her own French background. The desire to go back had grown. Now it was more than that. It had become an obsession.

"Don't you see, Luc, how important this is?"

Luc *did* understand. He was comfortable with his own dual heritage. He thoroughly enjoyed the summers he spent in France, spoke French fluently, loved everything French. He had unconsciously whetted Niki's appetite to explore her native country. But this thing about finding her birth parents was something even she must know was nearly impossible, given the mass confusion and chaos that was the aftermath of the war. Still, she had thought about it so much that it had become a possibility.

Cara soon saw that Niki could not be talked out of it. So Cara and Kip decided that, as a graduation present, they would allow Niki to accompany Luc when he left the first week in July. Niki had no idea Cara had to sell an heirloom set of jewelry, a cameo pendant and earrings, to finance her trip.

Kip drove Luc and Niki to Richmond to catch their train to New York. There they would stay overnight in Kitty and Craig Cavanaugh's Manhattan apartment. The following day Kitty and Craig would take the two young people to board the ship for their trip to France.

That evening Cara wandered alone through the house. She stopped at the door of Niki's empty, now perfectly neat bedroom. Standing in the doorway, she remembered the nights she had tucked her into bed and said with her the prayer she had learned herself at the same age, listened to the little girl, who still had the slightest French accent, repeat the words:

Matthew, Mark, Luke, John,
The bed be blest that I lie on,
Four posters to my bed
Four angels round my head
One to watch and one to pray,
Two to bear my soul away.

At this point Niki would always interrupt, saying, "Now let's say Luc's prayer." And she would repeat the one Luc had taught her—"Now I lay me down to sleep . . ."—the goodnight prayer that Kip had taught him. Even from the beginning Niki had wanted to copy everything Luc did.

Cara smiled wistfully in the dark. "God bless them both tonight, wherever they are." She closed Niki's door and Luc's as well. It was going to be a long summer.

chapter
2

Dear Tante and Uncle Kip,

Luc saw me into a taxi at the Gare du Nord, and he had to run to catch his own train to Provence. The bustle at the station was unbelievable. The porters shouting, the noise, the sooty smell, the honking of the cabs lined up at the curb. Everyone speaking French fast and loud. I could only catch a few sentences, phrases here and there. I didn't realize my French was so poor. I hope it will come back. After all, it was my first language—surely it will come back? I handed the driver the card with the name of the pension Aunt Kitty recommended, and we arrived safely.

Love,
Niki

Aunt Kitty had given Niki a small leather-bound notebook of blank pages, telling her, "You must keep a journal. Put down your impressions, a few words even, so when you get home, you can read it over and relive all those marvelous moments."

Niki had thanked her but had not thought she would use it very much. Aunt Kitty was a writer, so she always thought in terms of words.

Niki was usually too busy living whatever she was doing rather than writing about it. However, much to her surprise, when she got to France she found herself so filled with an emotional response to all she was seeing, things she knew she would want to remember, that she began to carry the little book with her, jotting down impressions on the spot. It also became a place where at the end of the day she wrote honestly about things she would never put in a letter home. Although she tried to write home at least once a week, there were many things she was thinking and feeling that might hurt Cara. She was beginning to be aware of the sense of being French, and her desire to seek some information about her parents had increased.

In her journal she wrote,

> I am in Paris. After writing those words, I can hardly believe it! A dream come true, a hope realized. I walk the streets wondering how my *real* mother felt. Am I seeing what she saw, feeling what she felt? Did she fall in love here? Will I?

For Niki everything was stimulating about Paris. She felt free, enormously happy here—as if she belonged. Even as she explored the streets, the byways, the little shops and the sidewalk cafes, all had a familiarity, as if she knew them from somewhere—in her bones, in her blood. Everything was here for her to discover; there was no veil over the past, nothing mysterious or hidden.

She tried to capture the essence of her experience in her letters and journal entries:

> *Ma chere Tante (I'm practicing writing in French!),*
>
> *My room is very nice—up steep steps, almost to the top of the house. I am sitting at a table looking out my window at the roofs and chimneys. From here I can see a small strip of*

gray that must be the Seine in the very far distance. I must explore everything. Today I am going to the Louvre. Au revoir—for now. More later.

Always,
Niki

I awake early, the gray, pink dawn rising over the city. I feel like I'm awakening not from a dream but into one. I am really here. The place of my birth and all those early unremembered years. I must go out and find myself.

I must celebrate, treat myself to something special. A Parisian bonnet, of course. Everyone must have a hat from Paris! I saw one that I admired in a milliner's shop the other day; now I think I must have it. It is hardly more than a scrap of feathers and a tiny nose veil. It is *"enchante,"* the salesperson declares. And I agree. I've never seen anything so ridiculous-looking. I'll probably give it to Scotty Cameron when I get home. She would love it and love to brag about having a hat from Paris to her snooty friends at boarding school, *n'est ce pas?* Meanwhile I shall wear it and enjoy my new image. Perhaps I'll wear it to attend High Mass at the Cathedral of Notre Dame, or something equally formal and appropriate.

Ma chere Tante,

What a wonderful surprise I had early yesterday morning. Luc showed up at the pension with Paul Duval! I hadn't seen him, of course, since the winter he spent with us at Montclair. He is much more handsome, sophisticated, than he was then. Maybe Frenchmen mature sooner than Americans. Anyway, Madame Genvieve, the concierge here, gave both of these tanned, good-looking "vagabonds" a severe look when they asked for me (Luc imitated her suspicious frown for me later), and when I came running downstairs, flung myself into Luc's arms, she almost fainted. I laughingly explained, "*C'est mon frere*" several times before she beamed a big smile and bustled about to serve them fresh coffee and croissants.

We had a marvelous day, the three of us. At noon in Paris everything stops. Shop doors post signs declaring they will be back in two hours, shutters are closed, bookstalls fold up. All along the riverbank Parisians relax, taking a leisurely lunch hour. We decided to join them. We bought loaves of the delicious bread they make here every day (I shall find it hard to eat ordinary bread ever again!), chunks of cheese, luscious peaches, and grapes for a picnic, and Paul bought a bottle of wine. Now, don't worry, Tante, I did not drink any. But for Paul, a Frenchman, it is the accepted thing. He says French children are weaned on it. Of course, I don't believe that for a minute. Or much of any of the other things Paul declared as fact when I asked him for some suggestions as to becoming more acclimated. I'm afraid half of what he tells me will get me into difficulties. He is a terrible tease— but also terribly charming. Luc looks on all this banter between us with indulgent good humor. Their plan is to go on to Holland, where they hope to find jobs as waiters and continue their bicycle trip through the Netherlands. It sounds so exciting. I wish I could go along. I hinted at the possibility but both of them ignored me. It is irritating to still be treated sometimes as an annoying little sister. Inside I feel very grown-up.

I still have Paris to discover, and although I hated for our day together to end, I saw them off the next day without feeling too bad. I will see them both at the end of the summer. In the meantime, today I am going back to the Louvre. Does anyone ever get enough of that?

chapter

3

Paris

NIKI'S HEART WAS THRUMMING as the taxi stopped with a jerk
in front of the gray, stone building behind tall, black iron gates.
On a metal plaque was engraved *Les Soeurs de Merci.* Niki
thrust several franc notes into the driver's grubby hand and
got out. For a few minutes she stood staring through the rungs
of the gate. Years ago another young woman—perhaps her
mother—had stood in the same place, a baby in her arms, the
child she was going to give up. What emotions had run
through her heart, mind? Niki's knees felt wobbly as she
approached the large brass bell with its leather pull that hung
to one side. With a shaky hand she gave it a tug. The gong
seemed to echo in the quiet summer afternoon. It seemed a
long time before she saw a figure wearing a brown cape, lowered head veiled in black, approach.

"*Comment?*" a low voice asked.

"*Bon jour,*" Niki said in a voice that sounded husky in her
tight throat. "*S'il vous plait,* I wish to speak to someone in
charge—the Reverend Mother?" Her mixture of English and
French sounded garbled to her own ears.

"*Seour Bernadine? Queue a vous?*"

"Nicole"—she hesitated—"Montrose. *J'ais Americaine.*" She wasn't sure why she had added that, except maybe someone here remembered Tante. Too late Niki remembered that back then Tante's name was Brandt. A war widow, she had been married to a young army chaplain, Owen Brandt.

"Une moment," the nun replied. She lifted the latch, opening the gate for Niki to enter. They crossed a sun-warmed cobblestone courtyard bordered with flowers, through a massive oak double door, and into a cool, dim interior. *"Assez vous."* The nun gestured to a carved wooden bench, then glided down the paved stone corridor and disappeared.

A few minutes later she returned, accompanied by the small, bent figure of another nun. As they approached, Niki saw a brown, wrinkled face peering from under the white wimple and flowing black veil. Tiny and stooped with age as she was, the woman exuded dignified authority that commanded respect. Immediately Niki stood up.

"*Bon jour.* I am Souer Bernadine, the Reverend Mother here. What can I do for you, *ma cher enfant*? Have you come to inquire about our novitiate?"

"*Non*, Soeur Bernadine," Niki replied quickly. "I was an orphan here, and I have come seeking some information about my real parents."

The nun's face underwent a change of expression. A look of deep compassion, the eyes full of sympathy.

"Ah, I do not know whether we can help you or not, *ma cher.* You must understand that, after the war, things were in such confusion. Records, birth certificates, that kind of thing, were often lost, or nobody had registered a baby. People fled to the country, and there no one was in charge. Everyone was so busy just trying to get their lives back together. There was so much to do. The children just had to be taken care of, housed, fed—" She saw Niki's look of disappointment and put

22

out a small, thin hand to her. "If you have a birth date, perhaps. We shall try. Come with me."

Niki followed the small figure down the hallways, then into a small room. The windows looked out onto the convent garden, where several nuns were walking in a slow circle, holding small black prayer books as they moved. She looked around what she assumed was Souer Bernadine's spartanly furnished office. A large crucifix hung on the wall, with a wooden *pre-dieu* before it. A large armoire took up most of the remaining wall space, and it was to this that Souer Bernadine went. She opened the doors to shelves of books, ledgers. Murmuring to herself, she examined the numbers on the spine of a few of them. Niki could see they were marked by years.

"You say *vous avais dix-oite ans, Cherie?*" the nun asked, turning to her.

"Yes, *oui,* at least I believe so, Souer," Niki replied.

Souer Bernadine pulled a large book labeled 1920 from under a stack and brought it over to her desk. She opened the heavy cover and started searching the pages, running one of her index fingers, gnarled as with arthritis, down the page.

"We had *beaucoup des enfants* brought in that year!" she said shaking her head and clucking her tongue. "Some were left just outside the gates, others brought in by who knows? Neighbors? A relative? Sometimes the mother herself. All with such sad stories." Souer Bernadine began to read the names: "Robert, Gillaume, François, Madeline . . . ah, here we have Nicole." The finger stopped and Niki leaned forward eagerly. "Nicole. *Mais,* there are several Nicoles—Dubois, St. Claire, Beauchampe, Gilbreaux . . ." The nun raised her head and fixed her shiny black eyes upon Niki. "We cannot be sure any of these names are *your* name, *Cherie.* Like so many of our orphans, it may be that someone—perhaps this person Gilbreaux—found you abandoned, or perhaps you were left with her by a parent who said she would be back, then never returned. These notations are never positive identification."

Gilbreaux. Niki repeated it to herself. *Nicole Gilbreaux.* For years in Mayfield she had been known as Niki Montrose. It would take some getting used to.

She thanked Soeur Bernadine for her time and trouble, then left. She walked for a long time without direction, her mind completely occupied with that day long ago when this mysterious person had carried the tiny, frail baby and left her at the orphanage among the other war orphans, to be cared for by generous sisters and volunteers. Volunteers like Tante. How strange it was that of all the babies in the orphanage nursery, Tante had taken her. How different her life would have been if—it was foolish to even consider what might have happened to her. As Souer Bernadine had said, so many babies, so many sad stories.

Ma chere Tante,

I cannot believe my time in Paris is almost up. I leave at the end of the week for England, where Luc will meet me the second week in September. Aunt Garnet wrote that she is sending her car and chauffeur to pick me up in London! What luxury after all these weeks of walking the streets and taking the Metro. Will write from Birchfields.

Avec amour toujours,
Nicole

Sitting at the little desk in her pension room, Niki folded the letter, placed it in an envelope, set it aside to mail later. Feeling suddenly despondent, she opened her journal to the page where, after visiting the orphanage, she had listed the names, one after the other: Nicole Dubois, Nicole St. Claire, Nicole Beauchampe, Nicole Gilbreaux—which was she? Who brought her to the orphanage? Her real mother? A friend? A relative? Who? She felt a sweeping despair. She had tried to learn more, checking any source she could think of for more information about her identity, but she had been continually frustrated. She would have to accept the fact that she might never know. But not yet. She would go on looking. There might not be any time left this summer, but Niki determined to come back next summer . . . and the summer after that . . . however long it took. . . .

chapter
4

Birchfields

THE PLAN HAD BEEN for Luc to meet Niki at Garnet's country house early in September, and then they would return to the States together. But Luc was hardly back in England before the dreaded news broke that England had joined France and was at war with Germany.

Luc's first thought was of his friend Paul, whom he had just left after returning from their summer together. Knowing Paul's fierce patriotism, Luc was sure he would not wait for conscription but would volunteer for military service immediately. *Liberté, Equalité, Fraternité.* The French were very proud of their democratic heritage. They would fight to maintain it. But no one, or only a few, had expected to have to fight for it again so soon.

Luc's heart and mind were troubled as he took the train down to Birchfields the second week in September. He was concerned not only for his friend but also for his elderly grandparents. Besides, he knew his parents would be worried about he and Niki getting safely home.

Afterward Luc told himself he should have been forewarned.

When he arrived at Birchfields, Aunt Garnet, after bidding him an affectionate hello, said, "Niki's waiting for you in the garden. I'm sure you two have lots to talk about. Go along. I'll see about tea."

Knowing Niki as well as he did, he should have guessed what she was going to tell him. Still, it came as a shock. After her usual enthusiastic hug and exuberant greeting, she looked at him directly and said, "Luc, I'm not going back!"

Luc stared at her. "What do you mean, you're not going back? Cara and Dad are frantic about you. They're trying to get Senator Maynard and Scott to pull all sorts of strings to get us home safely."

"I said I don't intend to leave," Niki repeated stubbornly.

"Are you out of your mind? There's a war on, Niki."

"That's just it, Luc. France, my country—and in a way yours—is at war. How can we go home as if nothing has happened, as if we aren't involved?"

"We're Americans, Niki. America's not at war."

"It will be. France and America are longtime allies. Think of the Revolution—both of them, the American and the French Revolutions. We always helped each other. Have you forgotten your history?"

Luc could think of no rebuttal to that. Seeing she had momentarily confounded him, Niki went on. "Don't you understand, Luc? I'm French! It's *my* country. I didn't realize it until this summer. The language came back, almost like magic. I *felt* French."

"I'm half French, too, you know," Luc said slowly. "I feel the same way, only perhaps not so strongly. If the United States is drawn into this—and they *could* be, as in the last war—then it makes sense to get involved. But not now, Niki. We've got to go home—"

"No, Luc. I'm not going." She shook her head stubbornly.

"What in the blazes do you think you can do?" he demanded.

"There are all sorts of possibilities. I'm not exactly sure just what. Join one of the women's special services."

"You're not old enough," Luc said flatly.

"That's not true. Nobody knows my real age. I don't have a birth certificate. Tante told me I was a baby when I came to the orphanage but was small because I was so undernourished. I could have been six months older than I looked. Maybe even older."

"But you're an American citizen. You can't join some branch of the English or French services."

"You don't know, I guess. Tante never followed through on my applying for citizenship. She thought that when she adopted me, I would automatically become a citizen." Niki shook her head, her dark curls bouncing. "But then she found out I had to apply for myself." She shrugged, a definitely Gallic gesture she had perfected during her summer, Luc thought, slightly amused. "So I am legally a French citizen."

Again Luc was silent. He crossed his arms, scowling at her, wishing he could come up with some inflexible argument. But at the moment none came to mind. Niki considered telling Luc about her search for her parents in Paris, how she had a clue that she had not been able to trace. If she had had more time, she might have been able to travel to Rouen, the city located on the Seine just north of Paris, to seek more information. But then she had to leave. She had planned to talk to Aunt Garnet, extend her stay in Europe, return to France to pursue her quest. Then before she could do anything, war had been declared.

Niki softened her tone and lowered her voice. "Don't you understand, Luc? I have to do something. I can't just sit here on my hands." Niki's dark eyes pleaded. "Aunt Garnet said I can stay here at Birchfields with her, help with her war work until I know for sure what I can do."

"Nursing?" Luc asked, thinking of Aunt Kitty.

"No, no! I'd be no good at that. I need something more active—"

"More adventurous, you mean. More risky, more dangerous."

"Maybe.

"Come on, Niki, you've got something up your sleeve. I know you too well. What's going on?"

"I could be an interpreter, for instance. They'll need people who can speak and understand French. This summer I barely spoke anything else. It all came back to me easily. I'd even begun to *think* in French. And that's the real test. The British will need people like me."

Luc's face became very serious. He knew she was right. People fluent in French would certainly be at a premium. But Niki wasn't a British subject. He had thought of her as an American. Now he knew differently. Why hadn't Cara ensured Niki's citizenship? If she had, they wouldn't be in this dilemma now. He knew Niki. She had a will of iron. He recalled one time she had sat at the dinner table until nine o'clock staring at a plate of turnips. Kip had insisted she at least try one, and she had refused. Luc smiled in retrospect. If they couldn't get the child Niki to eat something she didn't like, how did he expect to get her to come back to the United States once she had made up her mind?

Whatever the outcome of her military service application and no matter his powers of persuasion, Luc knew Niki was determined not to return to Virginia with him. But still he had to try.

"We've got our return tickets. They'll be expecting you to be with me," he said without too much conviction. "What will I tell them? How can I explain I've left you here?"

"I'll be perfectly fine here with Aunt Garnet until I see if I can get into one of the services," Niki said confidently. "She would love to have me. She says having young people around keeps *her* young!"

Luc rolled his eyes. "Are you sure she meant *you?* Young people like you are more likely to give adults gray hair."

Niki laughed gaily and Luc knew the battle was lost. He also knew he'd have a lot of explaining to do when he got to Montclair.

The Women's Royal Naval Service officer regarded Niki with mingled dismay and interest. She certainly wasn't run-of-the-mill, nor were her answers to the application questionnaire routine. The WRENS officer frowned, looked down at the sheaf of papers in the folder identified as Nicole Gilbreaux's.

"I see your education was in the United States, yet you were born in France," she said.

"Yes. You see, my real parents were—*are*—French. I was adopted by Americans. Mr. and Mrs. Kendall Montrose of Mayfield, Virginia."

"Ah, well, yes. Did you graduate from high school?"

"Yes."

"Have a college diploma?"

"No. I didn't—"

"So what qualifications do you have? Clerical skills?"

Niki thought of the summer she had worked with Cara-Lyn Maynard in the file room of the *Mayfield Messenger,* their Uncle Scott's newspaper. Boring, tedious, dreadful job! She sure didn't want to be stuck in the same kind of rut here if accepted in the WRENS. She shook her head. "No, not really."

The officer frowned. "Can you type?"

Niki hesitated. She did know how to type. That is, if you could call the hunt-and-peck system she had used on Luc's old portable for her themes and term papers. If she answered in the affirmative, would she land in some dull, dead-end clerk job? Would she lose the chance for a more interesting assignment if she admitted that she could use a typewriter? It was probably a toss-up.

The officer's frown deepened and she tapped her pen impatiently. Niki's innate honesty won out. "Yes, a little."

The officer marked something down, then started to close the folder. Desperate to make an impression before the interview was over, Niki blurted out, "I can speak and understand French." Seeing a spark lighten the officer's cold stare, she added, "Fluently."

"Indeed. Well, that does put another slant on things." The officer checked something on Niki's papers. "However, you must realize that until we have official confirmation of American citizenship or you are able to obtain a statement of your birth as a French national, there may be some delay in being able to place you in any of the women's services."

"Isn't there some way—"

"Certain rules have to be met. We understand your willingness to serve, and appreciate that. But"—the officer shrugged and closed the folder—"that's the way things work. I'm sorry."

On the train back to Birchfields, Niki went over and over the interview, trying to think how she could have handled it better. She hadn't thought her adoption would be such a stumbling block. The newspapers were always saying how great the needs were in all branches of the service. Here she was, eager and anxious to volunteer, and she was blocked at every turn. Her feeling of helplessness returned. She didn't really belong to anyone, didn't really belong anywhere. She couldn't even prove that she had been born. Would she have to go through her whole life an orphan, endlessly seeking her identity?

Back at Birchfields at teatime, Niki expressed her discouragement to Bryanne and Garnet.

31

"It's wartime and everyone keeps saying how much they need people, especially women, to release men for combat service, yet here I am, more than willing to serve, and I keep getting turned down."

Bryanne looked at her sympathetically. "I know it's hard, Niki, but they do have regulations they have to abide by, I guess."

"But it's ridiculous!" Niki's lower lip pushed out in a little pout.

"It's Cara's fault," Garnet said. "She should have seen that you applied for citizenship."

Niki rose quickly to her beloved mother's defense. "Don't blame Tante, please, Aunt Garnet. She assumed that by adopting me, I automatically became a citizen."

"Well, she should have made sure, looked into it. . . ." Garnet always had to have the last word.

Niki didn't want to agree with Garnet, who often found fault with everyone. Yet secretly she did resent Cara's not legally securing her American citizenship. It was typical of her careless ways. *Tante would never have let one of her horses go unregistered*, Niki thought morosely.

Garnet glanced at the young woman, saw the melancholy expression, then said to Niki, "Think of it this way, dear child—you are being of enormous help to us, to Bryanne and me, here at Birchfields. And we're doing a great deal for the war effort."

"Providing punch and coffee and dancing?" Niki retorted. "I don't think that helps much."

"You'd be surprised how much it means to the men, young lady," Garnet retorted, bristling. "To have a little fun, music, distraction, when most of the time their lives are so regimented, so intense. . . . Just ask any one of them. That is," she added sharply, "when you're not feeling so sorry for yourself."

Niki looked from Garnet to Bryanne. She saw something in their eyes that made her say contritely, "I'm sorry. I guess that's how I do come off. I know there are all sorts of ways to serve. I just wanted to—I don't know, do something more."

"More exciting, you mean?" Garnet gave her a knowing look.

"Yes, I think that's what I mean."

"Have you ever heard the quotation 'They also serve who only stand and wait'?" Garnet asked. "Change that to 'laugh, chat, and dance,' and you'll fill the bill."

Niki smiled, if rather grudgingly.

"So put on your prettiest dress and your best smile and make some of these lonely fellows who'll be coming over this weekend forget about the war for a little while."

Niki smiled back. "OK, I will."

Niki tried hard to take Garnet's advice. With her usual energy and enthusiasm, she threw herself into war-effort activities. She worked with Birchfields' head gardener, transforming some of the formal flower beds into vegetable gardens to provide produce for the community food bank. She volunteered for as many jobs as the local Red Cross group could assign. Busy as she was, however, there was still a longing within her to do something more.

1940

chapter

5

IN THE SUNNY DINING ROOM at Birchfields, Garnet settled herself at the table and picked up the newspaper folded at her plate. She opened it with a sense of dread. Lately the news had been devastating. Dunkirk had been a terrible blow. Under the relentless air attack of the Nazis, the Allied troops had retreated to the coast. Although there were naval ships offshore, they could not help the stranded troops, because they had no way to transport them. It was then the stalwart British had shown what they were made of. As soon as the plight of their soldiers was known, a volunteer fleet made up of every kind of craft available—privately owned dinghies, rowboats, yachts, pleasure boats—rushed to the rescue. It was an impossible task undertaken with the rallying cry that failure was unacceptable. The heroic effort succeeded, much to the astonishment of the world. The unarmed seamen made trip after trip to pick up the exhausted men and take them to the waiting ships. In the end some were taken prisoner by the advancing Germans. However, the gallant endeavor of ordinary people to save their defenders was universally hailed. Garnet felt pride in the valor of her adopted countrymen.

Today's headlines were dire, although security kept the newspapers very guarded in their reporting of just how bad the situation was. Would America get involved? As an American, Garnet wondered. The impression she had from her Virginia relatives was that the United States was increasingly isolationist. Having been drawn against their will into the last war—the one that was supposed to end all wars—there were many, like Kitty Cavanaugh, who adamantly opposed involvement.

Sighing, Garnet turned to the inside page to read "Grace Comfort's" column. She always read it tongue in cheek. Before it was revealed who Grace Comfort really was, Garnet had always scoffed at the saccharine content, at what she considered its overly sentimental style. But now that her stepniece, Lenora, was married to Victor Ridgeway, the *real* author, she read it regularly. Whatever her personal opinion of his subject, Garnet had to admit that he did strike a generally optimistic note that many found inspiring. Adjusting her glasses, she began to read. Soon, with a huff of indignation, she got up and walked into the hallway and picked up the phone and called the number of the Ridgeways' country home.

In the morning room at King's Grace, Lenora picked up the phone. "Good morning, Aunt Garnet. How nice of you to phone."

"I'm not sure you'll think so when you know why," Garnet replied.

"Why, what is it, Auntie?"

"I've just finished reading Grace's—I mean Victor's—column today, and I'm most upset about it."

"But why?"

"I assumed Grace's—*Victor's*—purpose was to lift people's spirits, to encourage. This is quite the opposite. Very negative. Quoting Edward Grey . . . listen to this: 'The lamps are going out all over Europe; we shall not see them lit again in our life-time.' If that isn't blatant defeatism, I don't know what is," Garnet declared.

There was a pause as she waited for Lenora to respond. "Well, Auntie, Victor is very depressed about the war. He was very much a supporter of the League of Nations after the last one, believed it to be the only hope for the world. If you read further than the first few paragraphs, though, you'll see he ends up quoting Winston Churchill."

"Hmmph." Garnet was loathe to admit she had not read the whole column.

"Victor is extremely patriotic, Aunt Garnet," continued Lenora. "He takes his work very seriously. From the number of letters he gets every day, I think he has the pulse of the nation. His mail is overwhelmingly positive."

A bit taken aback by having acted precipitously, an action more indicative of youth than of someone her age, Garnet conceded she would finish reading today's "Inspirational Moment."

Lenora replaced the receiver and turned to her younger sister, Lady Blanding, and lifted her eyebrows.

"I gather Aunt Garnet is at it again?" Lalage smiled. "Victor's column, I suppose?"

"Yes." Lenora shook her head. "You would think the old dear had enough to do running Birchfields without trying to editorialize Victor's column, wouldn't you?"

"I'm surprised she doesn't send daily communiqués to the War Office."

"Well, the poor old thing is probably lonely," concluded Lenora. "I thought her granddaughter Bryanne was planning to come stay with her. Especially since Bryanne's husband, Steven, went into the medical corps."

"Yes, she is lonely. But of course Niki is there."

"But probably not for long. She's trying desperately to get into one of the services."

"She's too young, isn't she?"

"I think it's not that. She hasn't got the right papers or something." Lenora reached for the silver teapot on the tray by her chair and asked, "More tea? No? Well then, suppose we discuss the fund-raising event? Let me get my list."

She rose and walked gracefully to the Louis XIV desk, while Lalage looked around the room with pleasure. The morning room at King's Grace reflected the exquisite taste of its mistress. When Lenora had married the wealthy journalist Victor Ridgeway, he had given her carte blanche to decorate the old country place he had bought and lived in for some years as a bachelor. Its pale ivory woodwork, brocaded draperies, the lemon-and-lime color scheme, was a fitting background for her delicate, blond beauty. There were Chinese rugs, thick and patterned in blue and jade. There were rounded, velvet-covered sofas and club chairs grouped conversationally around the white marbled fireplace.

The sun rested benignly on the two silver blond heads as they bent over the list. The society columns had often described them as the "beautiful American sisters" when they had both married Englishmen in 1897, the year of Queen Victoria's Jubilee. And though both were now in their fifties, they were still so described.

As they sipped their Darjeeling tea and nibbled cucumber sandwiches, they got to the business at hand. When they had worked out the details of the fete they were planning to hold at Blanding Court, the ancestral home of Lalage's husband, they talked of more serious things.

"Is Neil truly worried about an immediate crisis?" Lenora asked worriedly.

"Well, you know him—he's always inclined to take the most

cautious view of things. He always felt that the government should have taken stronger steps sooner to combat the aggression of that awful Hitler. But he was one of those voices crying in the wilderness." Lalage shook her head. "Now, of course, we have Chance to worry about." She was referring to her twelve-year-old son. "Even though he's just in the fourth form at his school, he hopes the war lasts long enough for him to go. Imagine. As he is the heir to the family estate, we can all fervently hope it will be over long before that." She looked over at her sister. "You really ought to be grateful you don't have any boys, Lenora."

"I don't know about that. Victor would have loved to have a son...."

"Well, I must be on my way," Lalage said, rising and gathering her purse, gloves, and hat. "Alair and Cilla are waiting for me to help with the children's picnic they planned for this afternoon." Refugee children sent from London to escape the German bombing were now staying at Blanding Court. She kissed her sister good-bye and left.

Garnet put on her glasses again and finished reading Grace Comfort's column. "No matter how great the odds, we British heartily support Winston Churchill's promise: 'We shall fight on the beaches, we shall fight on the landing grounds, we shall fight in the fields and in the streets, we shall fight in the hills; we shall never surrender.'"

chapter

6

ON A SATURDAY EVENING late in July, Niki got ready for the regular weekend open house at Birchfields. For some reason she felt less eager than ever to spend hours chatting and dancing. In spite of all her volunteer activities, she still couldn't shake the restlessness she felt to be part of something bigger.

She put on the dress she had found at one of those obscure Paris boutiques where fabulous fashion bargains are possible. It was a silk print scattered with daisies, bluebells, and poppies, the wildflowers of French country fields. It had cap sleeves, a scoop neckline, flared skirt, and set off Niki's petite figure flatteringly. Her hair had grown to shoulder length, and she tied it back with a scarlet ribbon.

She was downstairs when the first contingent of servicemen from the airfield began to arrive. Since the Dunkirk disaster there had been some foreigners among them, some who had managed to escape from countries overrun by the Nazis and were now training with British units in England.

Alair Blanding and Cilla Ridgeway had come over from Blanding Court for the weekend to help with hostessing. The cousins and Niki had become friends over the past few months. Cilla was still at boarding school, but Alair was helping at the village school. The facility had been taxed to overflowing by the sudden influx of refugee children from London. With the relentless nightly bombing raids, many parents had sent their children to the country for safety. Blanding Court had several of the children, with their teachers, billeted in the house. Some mothers of the smaller children had accompanied them and helped at the school.

Alair had volunteered to take over the kindergarten. As she dearly loved children and her sweet, quiet nature was perfect for such a job, she was busy during the week. She loved coming to Birchfields to assist at the weekend open house. She laughingly said, "It gives me a chance to talk with adults for a change. I spend most of my waking hours with tots under age five, and I'm afraid my vocabulary is shrinking as a result."

Both girls were lovely, slender blonds with English-rose complexions, and were immensely popular as dance partners. Niki watched them almost enviously. Obviously enjoying themselves, they both had found their niche and were satisfied that they were doing their part.

That evening Niki tried to appear cheerful. But inside she was still depressed about her fruitless interview with the WRENS recruiting officer. No matter how Bryanne and Aunt Garnet tried to encourage her, Niki still worried that she would never have enough official clearance to get into any of the services. She felt particularly drawn to the WRENS, the women's branch of the Royal Navy.

"A penny for your thoughts," a deep, accented voice spoke.

Knowing it was somehow familiar, Niki slowly turned around. She saw a handsome face she recognized. Deeply tanned, leaner, older, but those dark, mischievous eyes, the slightly ironic smile, were unmistakable. It was Paul Duval, Luc's French companion. Her gaze swept over him. The black curly hair that used to fall across his forehead in waves and curl around his ears and neck was now clipped in a military cut; the mouth, with its curve of humor, was now shadowed by a mustache. But still it was Paul, the boy she had daydreamed about, the young man who had ignored her, until . . . last summer in Paris . . .

"Paul!"

"*Cherie!*" he responded with a broad smile. "Niki! Yes, *c'est moi*!" He caught her up in a quick hug, kissing her on each cheek, and swung her around before setting her down again. Still holding her around the waist, he gazed at her with delight. "Are you surprised?"

"Of course, I'm flabbergasted! But how did you get here? We've been so worried. Luc's written me a dozen times, asking if there was any word of you. . . ."

"I got out with some of the last from Dunkirk. Here I was reassigned to what remained of my unit. I've been training . . . but enough about me. What are you doing here in England? I thought you went home with Luc last September."

"Come, I'll tell you all about it." Niki took his arm. "Let's find a place where we can talk."

There was so much to talk about, so much to share. First Niki took Paul to meet Aunt Garnet, to explain who he was and how dear he had become to the family in Virginia. Then she introduced him to Bryanne and Alair and Cilla. Aunt Garnet insisted he stay at Birchfields instead of going back to the airfield, where he had temporary quarters.

"You are very kind, but I cannot."

"How long will you be at the airfield?" she asked.

A curious, shuttered expression passed over Paul's face. He murmured something about waiting for reassignment. Garnet, who understood wartime security, immediately said, "Of course, but you must come as often as you can get away. Any friend of Luc's is certainly welcome at Birchfields."

Paul glanced at Niki, who was looking at him eagerly. For a

split second something passed between them that made Niki draw in her breath. Then Paul smiled and, bowing slightly to Garnet, said, "You are most gracious, Mrs. Devlin. I accept your hospitality with thanks. *Merci.*"

During the next few weeks Paul was often at Birchfields. Sometimes he showed up without advance notice. He was always there on the weekends. The time she spent with Paul was like a dream come true for Niki. All her girlish fancies about Luc's fascinating French friend were playing out as from some predestined plan. The Paul she had fantasized about was a reality.

In the years since he had been at Montclair, he had attended the university, acquired a sophistication, an urbanity far beyond that of an American of the same age. Whatever he had been through in the short but savage war France had waged, about which he did not speak, had also given him a maturity that a less experienced young man would not have. Yet underneath he was genuinely sweet, surprisingly sensitive and sincere. When he and Niki were together, they spoke of many things they both enjoyed and a great deal about Paris.

"How I would love to show you Paris. It is particularly beautiful in the spring—" Here Paul's eyes would glaze a little, and a look of loss would pass over his face. Niki would try to bring him back to the present, making some remark about the future. Surely one day they would explore Paris together. Now it seemed enough that they were enjoying this English summer.

Paul talked little about what he had been through in the last, disillusioning days of France or about his time since its fall. He worshiped Charles de Gaulle, now the leader of the Free French, and of course despised Pétain, the WWI hero turned traitor, who headed the government at Vichy that collaborated with the Nazis. When Niki tried to draw him out on his thoughts of the future, he begged off. "Let's enjoy the moment, *Cherie,*" he would say and quickly change the subject. They did talk about Luc. Niki told him Luc was in the U.S. Army officers' flight training program in Texas. "I think he wishes now he'd stayed when I did, gone into the British Royal Air Force. He already has a pilot's license. He hopes America will join the Allies, if it's not too late—"

"There'll be time enough," Paul said. "I'm afraid it's going to take a while to defeat the Nazis . . . as my country learned to its regret."

"*My* country, too, Paul. Remember?" Niki said softly.

"Of course, *Cherie*. Now I do remember. I had forgotten. You seem so American."

"I do?" Niki looked disappointed.

Paul threw back his head and laughed. "French, American, who cares? You are adorable." He leaned over and touched the tip of her nose with his index finger.

One Saturday evening several weeks later, Birchfields was crowded. It seemed to Niki more servicemen than ever had flooded through the gates and filled the house. They were also several hostesses short. Cilla had gone back to school, and Alair had a cold, so neither had shown up to help. Niki and Bryanne and a few local girls did their best. Stationed at the punch bowl, Niki couldn't get away long enough to be with Paul as much as usual. By midnight, men with early-morning duties began to leave. Others drifted off to escort home some of the hostesses who lived in the village. Finally the bus left to take the rest of the servicemen back to the base.

Niki looked around, afraid that Paul, seeing she was busy, might have gone without saying good-bye. Then she saw him and, relieved, she went to him. He smiled and said, "I've waited all evening to have a dance with you."

Bryanne and one of the servants were going about extinguishing lights and pulling back the blackout curtains in the rooms that no longer needed to be darkened.

"Let's go outside. It's a beautiful evening," Paul suggested. Holding Niki's hand, he led her through the library, where a few people remained. Several airmen, not wanting to see their brief respite end, taking their chances of hitching a ride or walking back to the base, lingered still, gathered by the phonograph.

The moon was rising above the treetops, illuminating the garden.

"Bomber's moon," Paul muttered. "Poor London."

They both stood there, momentarily anticipating the whine of German bombers that would soon be roaring overhead on their way to send death and destruction on that beleaguered city. Then through the open doors the sound of dance music floated.

Paul took Niki in his arms, and they began dancing slowly to a popular ballad she loved. Paul was singing the lyrics in French, but Niki also knew them in English:

Long ago and far away
I dreamed a dream one day
and now that dream is here beside me.

Niki's heart quickened. She closed her eyes, following Paul's lead. They moved across the brick terrace as smoothly as if it were a polished dance floor. It *was* like a dream, she thought, almost imagining they were in Paris and all this was happening at another time . . . a time of peace, when anything was possible . . .

Paul whispered something, and slowly Niki moved back to reality. He had said something about having to go.

"So soon?" she asked dreamily.

He gave a low chuckle. "It is late, *Cherie*. I must go."

There was something in the way he said it that caused her heart to tighten—something almost final about it.

"But you'll be back next weekend?" she asked, as if needing reassurance. When he didn't reply, she prompted, "Promise?"

"Niki, in wartime there are no promises, no farewells, only *au revoir,*" Paul said gently.

Niki felt as if two cold hands were squeezing her heart. She started to ask something more, but Paul pressed two fingers against her lips, keeping her from saying it. Then he kissed her, not on each cheek in the traditional friendship manner of the French, but on her mouth. It was a kiss of great tenderness, but in it was a sadness, a relinquishment of what might have been in some other time or place.

Paul did not return to Birchfields. Niki carefully questioned some of the airmen who continued to come to the weekend gatherings, and learned that a small group of French officers had gone from the base. Rumor had it they had been sent on some kind of secret assignment. The surmise was that they had gone to join General de Gaulle in North Africa.

Paul's departure left an unexpected void in Niki's life. Was she in love with him? She certainly had been swept away by his glamor. He was strikingly handsome in his French officer's uniform, and his accent, his charm, were so different from the American boys she had known and dated in Virginia. It had certainly been a romantic interlude, but love? Niki wasn't sure.

1941

chapter

7

Mayfield, Virginia
Spring 1941

LYNETTE MONTROSE MAYNARD always felt an emotional tug when approaching Avalon. A sudden quickening of her heart, a sting of tears, a tightening of her throat. Its old brick-and-timber structure, the arched entrance overhung with climbing roses, all brought back the magical childhood she had spent there with her brother and sister, a childhood that had ended cruelly and abruptly with the death of their mother, Faith, in the *Titanic* disaster. The aftermath of the tragedy had split up their little family. Lynette had gone to the care of their grandmother, Blythe Cameron, in Virginia. Her baby sister, Bryanne, had gone to their other grandmother, Garnet Devlin, in England. Their brother, Gareth, had led a peripatetic life, moving about from place to place, living in New Mexico with their father, Jeff Montrose, a well-known artist, part of the year and going away to boarding school nine months of the year.

Providentially, somehow they had all survived.

At eighteen Gareth had rebelled, left college, declaring he had spent most of his life in school and now wanted to find out for himself what he wanted to do. He had chosen to come back to Avalon, the family home, situated on a small island across the river from Arbordale, Virginia. Their romantic parents had created a kind of enchanted world for themselves there and brought their children up on the legends of King Arthur and the Knights of the Round Table. Gareth was living out that legacy. A bachelor at thirty-two, he seemed perfectly content to remain on the isolated estate. He had become a landscape architect and ventured away from Avalon only as necessary for business. The rest of the time, he seemed to enjoy his solitary existence in his own woodland kingdom.

Lynette skillfully maneuvered the small boat she had rowed across from the ferry landing at Arbordale. She tossed the rope around one of the pilings and, coiling it securely, climbed up on the wooden dock.

A path of flat stepping-stone, bordered by a glorious abundance of white alyssum, pink phlox, purple lobelia, made a winding walkway up to the house.

"Gareth!" Lynette called. "It's Lynette! Where are you?"

A few minutes later a tall man in stained overalls, wearing leather gardening gloves and holding a large pair of pruning shears in one hand, emerged from around the side of the house.

"Well, Sis!" he greeted her with a wide grin. "To what do I owe a visit from the wife of our eminent state senator? An official inspection tour? Checking up on your recalcitrant brother?"

"None of the above!" She made a dismissing gesture. "I'm here on business, actually. Aren't you going to invite me in? Where are your so-called host manners?"

"I'm much too dirty to suggest we go inside. How about the grape arbor?" He gestured toward a rustic arch nearby, its latticed sides heavy with twining grapevines, and they walked over to it. "Business or no business, I'm glad you came," he said, indicating a seat. Then, almost as an afterthought, he asked, "What kind of business?"

"We have a job for you," Lynette said, brushing off the seat before sitting down. "Frank is going to rent Shadowlawn, his family's house in Arbordale. The yard badly needs tending. We've been in Richmond so much of the time and spent so many weekends out at Spring Hill. It's been in the hands of a realty firm, and they've been showing it for possible sale, but nobody seems to have the money these days. Frank doesn't like the idea of renting it to just anybody, but the realtor has come up with a good tenant, and we have agreed to a six-month lease. But the yard needs to be cared for—hedges trimmed, lawn mowed, everything tidied up. The renter will be here at the beginning of next month. Do you think you can have it ready by then?"

"Sure. I'll take a look at the place, of course, see what it needs. But probably a week will be enough time."

"Frank and I won't be here when they come, so will you take care of it for us?"

Gareth nodded. "Done."

"Good. Thank you, Gareth. That's one thing off my mind."

"You have a great many things burdening you, Sis?"

"Just the usual. Social things, mostly. Frank's colleagues and constituents, too." Lynette sighed as she got to her feet. "Well, I really must be off. I've shopping to do and errands to run."

"I'll walk to the ramp with you."

"Yes, do. I don't really understand why you continue to live out here by yourself, Gareth." She gave a little shudder. "It has too many memories for me. Even for father. So why do you?"

"I don't mind memories. Most of mine are happy ones. Except, of course, mother's death. I'm far happier here than I ever was away at school or in New Mexico." Gareth made a sweeping gesture with one arm. "Besides, I love this place."

"And being alone?" his sister persisted. "Don't you ever want to meet someone and fall in love? How do you expect anyone to share your castle with you when you isolate yourself on this island?" Lynette regarded her brother with a mixture of bewilderment and pique. "I've invited you dozens of times to events where there were any number of attractive young ladies, but you always refuse or don't show up."

"Don't worry about me, Sis. When the time is right, the right person will come along. Until then I'm perfectly happy, content."

"I hope you won't end up a crotchety old bachelor," she said, frowning.

Gareth laughed. "I'm sure you'll see that I don't—at least the crotchety part. Thanks for all your concern, Sis. But honestly, I'm doing just fine. Tell Frank I'll see to Shadowlawn, not to worry." He helped her into the boat and untied the rope. "By the way, who did you say is renting it?"

"I didn't say. The realtors handled the transaction, and Frank's secretary saw to the details." Lynette unlocked the oars and gripped them. "It's a missionary, just returned from Japan. Been ill, I understand, needs rest and quiet. Shadowlawn will be the perfect place for that."

A few days later, in Arbordale on business of his own, Gareth went to Shadowlawn to see what needed to be done to the yard. Lynette had given him the key, asking him to go inside and make sure that the house cleaners she hired had done a good job.

Arbordale had developed and grown in the other direction, so this part of town had very few houses. Most were very old, rundown, and spaced widely apart on a meandering country lane. The Maynards' family home, a simple, unpretentious colonial, was set back from the road on a large, overgrown lawn shaded by ancient trees. *At least it came by its name rightly,* Gareth thought as he got out of his pickup and looked around. Scraggly rhododendron bushes lined either side of the driveway, and the front porch was heavily hung with wisteria, nearly obscuring the entrance.

Gareth walked all around the house. The grounds needed a lot of work, he observed. This was more than a matter of simply mowing the grass and trimming the overgrown shrubbery. But that was about all he could accomplish before his sister's tenant came. He went up on the porch and let himself inside. At once the combined smells of astringent cleaners, furniture wax, floor polish—the residue of the house cleaners—made him sneeze. He could report to Lynette that a thorough job had been done.

A center hall ran the length of the house. The rooms were on different levels. On one side two steps led down into a large parlor; on the other side was a dining room. A staircase composed of a short flight of steps, a landing with a balcony, and then a longer flight of steps led up to the second floor, where the bedrooms were.

The rooms were sparsely furnished. Lynette had taken some of the better pieces and antiques to Spring Hill. As he walked through the downstairs, Gareth decided it had a peaceful feel, probably just right for the quiet, uncomplicated life—a good place for a recovering invalid.

Gareth worked most of the next weekend at Shadowlawn. He uncovered some flower beds that had been nearly eclipsed with weeds. As a professional, he saw what a beautiful place Shadowlawn could be if properly cared for. Maybe another day he could come back, if there was time.

Busy with his own spring planting, he did not get back to the Maynard place that week. In checking the calendar the following week, he couldn't recall the exact arrival date of the tenant. He hoped he hadn't missed it. Feeling somewhat guilty that he hadn't accomplished everything he knew needed doing, he decided to take some flowers from his own garden over to Shadowlawn, place them in vases in the house as a welcoming gesture.

It was late afternoon when he pulled into the driveway of Shadowlawn. To his dismay he saw there were lights on inside. He was too late. Somehow he had missed the time of arrival.

He got out of his pickup and, carrying two bouquets of mixed flowers, walked toward the house, then halted. He saw a figure standing at one of the long, open French windows at the side of the house, a woman in some kind of flowing robe.

It was an enchanting picture. For a few minutes he stood, captivated by the graceful silhouette created by the light of the room behind her. Then someone spoke to her and she half turned, so that Gareth saw her profile. He was struck by its perfection.

"Thank you," he heard her say. Her voice was low, rather husky. Immediately he thought of the Shakespeare line "Her voice was ever soft, gentle and low, an excellent thing in a woman."

Not wanting to startle her, thinking she would be frightened if she saw the figure of a man lurking in the yard, he approached the porch and called out, "Good evening! I'm Gareth Montrose, Mrs. Maynard's brother. I came to see if everything was all right."

There was a moment's hesitation. "Why, yes, thank you. That is very kind of you and Mrs. Maynard, of course." He still could not see her features clearly. "Please, won't you come in?"

In a few long strides he was at the bottom of the porch steps. She turned on the porch light and stepped out. When he saw her clearly, her beauty almost took his breath away.

She was the most exquisite creature he had ever seen. Her skin was as translucent as porcelain, her eyes a violet blue. Her hair grew from a point above her forehead and fell on either side of her heart-shaped face to her shoulders.

Gareth was not an artist's son for nothing. Growing up surrounded as he had been with paintings, art books, artists, he compared her beauty to that of one of the models used by Rossetti—Jane Burden, perhaps.

Was *this* Lynette's tenant? When she had said the person was a missionary returned to the States from Japan, Gareth had not thought to ask if it was a man or a woman. Somehow he had assumed it would be a male missionary, probably a man with a family, on furlough from his work in a foreign land.

Gareth's conjecture was interrupted when the woman said, "How kind of you to come." Her speech was very precise, almost as if English were her second language. She spoke slowly, as if choosing each word carefully. "Yes, indeed, everything was fine. We got here this afternoon and found all in order. Thank you."

We? Gareth wondered automatically. A husband? He felt a prick of dismay. Just then, from behind her, a diminutive young woman dressed in a blue-and-white striped cotton kimono suddenly appeared. She was, he saw, an Oriental— Japanese, of course.

"May I introduce my companion, Mitsuiko Yatasami."

Ah, the "we," Gareth thought with relief.

"Nice to meet you both. I brought these," Gareth said, handing over the bouquets to the young woman, who took them and withdrew. He stood there feeling a bit awkward. Then, as if he needed to explain, he said, "Your garden needs work, and I plan to get it in shape for you."

"How lovely and how very thoughtful of you, Mr. Montrose," she said. "And I think I forgot to introduce myself." She gave a melodic laugh. "I'm Brooke Leslie."

Gareth would always remember that moment, when he heard her name for the first time. It was as though everything suddenly receded and only that image of her remained. Her voice struck some unknown chord within him, a remembered echo of something he had been searching for all his life and was on the brink of finding. Whatever was happening, he could not quite grasp nor understand it.

Driving back from Arbordale, he could remember little of their conversation other than that he had assured her he would be available should she need anything. He hoped he hadn't said anything incredibly stupid. She was so utterly composed, so poised, that he simply found himself dazed. He had never felt like that before.

Gareth had never had a serious romance. Still, that evening he knew that he had met someone who would change his life forever.

The very next day Gareth brought vegetables from the garden at Avalon—lettuce, tomatoes, cucumbers. Mitsuiko took them, smiling and bowing. Miss Leslie was resting, she told him in her tiny voice. Although disappointed, Gareth said not to disturb her and left.

Back in his pickup, he felt like driving out to Spring Hill to question his sister, find out more about Brooke Leslie. She was so unlike anyone he'd ever met before, so different from his sisters, his cousins, any of the young women he was sometimes pressed to escort to social events he could find no excuse to avoid. He wondered what lay behind that quiet mask, her thoughtful, quiet ways too mature, too reserved, for her years.

Why hadn't Lynette informed him that the person renting Shadowlawn was someone so . . . But then he remembered Lynette saying that a realtor had made the arrangements, that neither of them had met the tenant. In a way, Gareth would like it just as well if his sister—or any of the family, for that matter—did not know about Brooke. They would all come rushing over with all sorts of tokens of Southern graciousness. Not that he didn't value that in his womenfolk. It was just that

Brooke was—well, different. To be truthful, he wanted to keep her to himself for a while, like some precious jewel he had come upon. Gareth shook his head in self-ridicule. *I'm going over the wall,* he thought.

Nevertheless, more and more he found himself leaving the island, rowing over to the mainland, inventing errands, reasons to go by Shadowlawn. His primary excuse was a commitment to get the garden in shape. Actually, he was doing more than he had at first intended.

One sweltering afternoon he had been working hard, weeding and thinning and transplanting some bulbs, when he heard his name called. Wiping his forehead with the back of his arm, he turned to see Brooke Leslie standing on the porch.

"Mr. Montrose, surely it's much too warm for all that. Can you stop and join me in a glass of lemonade?"

He was too hot and sweaty to sit on the chintz-pillowed wicker chairs, he told her. Instead he sat on the steps, and they had their first real conversation.

"I thought Virginia might be too warm for me this summer. But this place is so shaded, I've found it lovely and cool."

"This is the first time you've come here?" Gareth was avid with curiosity about her but was reluctant to ask too many questions.

"No, I came here to boarding school."

"In the States?"

"Yes, to North Carolina. My parents were teachers at a missionary school in Japan. By their teens, most missionaries' children are sent home for their education. It is an accepted practice. But I was an only child, and most of my friends were Japanese girls I'd known all my life, so I was terribly homesick. I missed Japan very much, found it difficult to adjust. I stayed just long enough to finish my high school education and then went home."

There was so much more Gareth wanted to ask, but he was too shy, afraid she might think him too probing.

Just then Mitsuiko glided onto the porch, bowing and apologizing, and told Brooke a package had been delivered for which she had to sign, so whatever else Brooke might have told him about herself was interrupted.

After that day, sharing iced tea or lemonade became a ritual they enjoyed almost every afternoon he worked in the garden at Shadowlawn. It was something Gareth looked forward to eagerly.

Soon the yard and garden were in good shape, requiring only a cutting and trimming once a week. Late one afternoon Gareth found himself restless, wanting to see Brooke Leslie, wondering if somehow he could drop by with some kind of plausible excuse. He racked his brain for some explanation, then decided he'd not even try to make something up. Impulsively he cut a huge bouquet of peonies and drove into Arbordale. As luck would have it, Brooke was lying on the wicker lounge out on the lawn. Because of the leafy maples, the lawn got the shade of the afternoon and was pleasantly cool.

She seemed delighted with the flowers and invited him to stay for iced tea. He drew up one of the lawn chairs and sat down, thinking how exquisite she looked in a peach-colored dress of some floaty material, her dark hair resting against blue-striped pillows.

Mitsuiko brought a tray with a pitcher of tea and tall frosted glasses with wedges of lemon, poured each of them a glass, then glided quietly away.

"I received a lovely note from your sister, my landlady, Mrs. Frank Maynard," Brooke said, smiling. "She said she would come by when the state legislature takes a recess and she and her husband come home for their summer vacation. I look forward to meeting her."

"Yes, Lynette is a great girl," Gareth agreed. "I think you'll like her. Makes a perfect politician's wife. You know, gracious, smiling, diplomatic."

A slight frown drew Brooke's dark feathery eyebrows together on her smooth brow. "That is unlike Japan. Political wives in Japan are rarely seen. For that matter, wives never socialize with their husbands in Japan. They live very separate existences. Except at home, of course . . ." She paused. "It is a very different culture."

"Tell me about Japan," Gareth prompted. He wanted to know everything about Brooke, where she had lived, what she had experienced. There wasn't anything about her he considered unimportant or trivial.

She began slowly to tell him. "Japan is a very beautiful country. Very different from America. Even though I'm an American, somehow I feel Japan is my heart's home. I grew up there, you see, and learned to love it, its people, its customs, at a very early age. I believe those first impressions when a child is still being formed are most important, don't you?"

Gareth thought of his own early childhood at Avalon, followed by all the years of confusion, uprooting, adjusting to different places, circumstances. Then at twenty-three he'd gone back to live at Avalon by himself. So he thought he understood what Brooke was saying. In a way Avalon was his "heart's home."

"There is a strange, wild, dark beauty in the Japanese landscape. You see it, of course, in their paintings—the stroke, the grays, the wash of a black line across white paper, indicating what the imagination can provide. Perhaps it is the mountains always in the background."

"You talk about it as though—" He paused, not knowing exactly why but feeling some anxiety stir within him.

A thoughtful expression crossed Brooke's face. Her eyes had a faraway look as she said, "As though I miss it? Yes, I do.

Although, I've tried to train myself to live in the moment, as the Quakers advise. To be present where you are." She paused and smiled. "And right now there is a great deal of change happening in Japan. A nationalistic spirit that is very strong. The military is influential, and after the war with China many factions are vying for power." She sighed. "Of course, in the countryside and where I was in the mountains it remains simple, peaceful. That is what I miss."

They both fell silent. It was not an uncomfortable silence but a companionable one, as two kindred spirits might enjoy. Fireflies flitted in and out of the bushes, blinking their little lights and creating a magical illusion. Finally Gareth said, "I want to show you my garden. I want you to see Avalon."

"I'd love to sometime."

Gareth wanted to set a day and time to do that right then but resisted. After all, Brooke was supposed to be recuperating from her illness, whatever it was, and it did not seem appropriate to push her into making a commitment.

chapter

8

BROOKE REALIZED SHE had begun to look forward to Gareth Montrose's visits. Warned to be careful, she had been inactive so long that she had started comparing herself mythically to Tennyson's wistful Lady of Shallot, who saw life only as a reflection in the mirror above her loom. But Gareth's vigorous, alive presence was making a difference; she was using this metaphor less and less. She could feel his energy, his vitality, his strength. In spite of warning herself not to become dependent, she had begun to anticipate his arrival.

It was only once in a while that she worried a little that his feelings for her might be growing deeper than friendship, perhaps even becoming romantic. But she ignored it. She didn't want anything to disturb this pleasant relationship. Why not enjoy this attractive, interesting young man's company? After all, she wouldn't be here that long. She had only signed a six-month lease.

But Brooke was a sensitive, introspective woman—or had become so in her long illness, the nature of which she had not fully disclosed to Gareth. In her years in Japan, Brooke had absorbed something of the Oriental stoicism, the reluctance to reveal personal problems. Possibly there was an even deeper reason why she had not discussed her condition with Gareth, one she found hard to admit even to herself.

She was afraid. Her illness had once robbed her of a happiness she had felt sure was hers. She had been young, just nineteen, recently returned to Japan, hopeful, idealistic, romantic. She met Justin Wilburn, a young missionary newly out of seminary. He had been full of zeal for the life he had chosen, and he wanted Brooke to share it. She had fallen in love with him almost at once, long before he expressed a similar attraction to her. They spent hours together, reading the Bible, discussing it—well, not really discussing, because Justin expounded on it to her. He was working as an assistant in the local church while awaiting a mission assignment from his denomination's missionary board in the States. Knowing that Justin's appointment would be enhanced if his wife were a trained nurse, Brooke entered nurses' training school at the American mission hospital. Upon her graduation they could marry and go into the mission field as a team.

The rigorous training had been physically too much for Brooke, and she had collapsed. She was diagnosed with tuberculosis. The treatment of choice then was complete bed rest, isolation in a mountain sanitarium. No visitors were allowed, because the disease was considered highly contagious.

Brooke had tried to be brave, had tried to believe that this was somehow part of God's plan for her life, that there was something important for her to learn from this. All during the long months as she lay in bed on the sanitarium's screened porch, bundled against the cold, clear mountain air, Brooke prayed for patience. She clung to the faith that eventually she would be healed so she and Justin could go on with their plans.

But that didn't happen. Fifteen months crept by, and then she received two letters. The first was a short one from Justin, saying only that he had received his assignment and would be leaving Japan for Kenya on the next ship. The second letter was from her mother, breaking the news as kindly as possible

that Justin was marrying a woman missionary who had recently arrived in Japan, that they had been seeing each other since
shortly after Brooke had been taken to the sanitarium.

Brokenhearted as she had been at the time, Brooke did not
blame Justin. She had always known that she had come second
to his life's calling, the Lord's work. She had been an asset only
as she could fulfill and support his vocation. Now that she could
no longer share that goal, he had to be free. Slowly she began
to understand and feel less and less sorry for herself. Perhaps if
she and Justin had married, it would have been a disaster—
maybe she would have failed him, maybe her health would have
broken later in Africa. There were a hundred maybes. . . .

In the end she admitted that God's ways are not our ways and
that maybe some other role was hers to play. When she improved
and was released from the hospital, she returned to her parents'
home. She began to teach private English lessons, tutoring stu-
dents who were going to the States for special education. Soon
she had other challenges to face. Brooke had been a late child
of middle-aged parents. Now they were both aging and in fail-
ing health. Eventually both died and Brooke was alone. A year
after their deaths Brooke had a relapse and was hospitalized for
a short period. It was during this time that she decided to come
to the States and seek further medical treatment.

The American doctor, a medical missionary who had known
her parents, was the one who had suggested that she see a col-
league of his at the university hospital in his native state of
Virginia, then spend a few months there for rest and relaxation.

Going over all that had happened to her, Brooke wondered if
it had all been for some purpose. Was it so that she would come
to Arbordale and meet Gareth Montrose? Nothing happens by
chance for a Christian. Everything that comes into a person's life
does so by God's permissive will. It seemed ironic that she would

travel all this way and see the possibility of happiness and love so far from the land she had come to think of as her own.

But to love Gareth and to allow him to love her was too dangerous. It would mean taking too great a chance. And always there was the risk of her health. She could not be a real wife to any man now. Especially to someone like Gareth, a man of the outdoors, a man of strength, and younger than she at that. A man who would certainly want a family . . . something Brooke could never give him. She had been told earlier, even when she was still quite young, that childbearing might kill her. This was her secret sorrow.

The weeks of summer passed in enjoyable companionship. Gareth brought flowers and vegetables from his abundant gardens at Avalon, and Brooke always asked him to stay for some refreshment, served by the shyly smiling Mitsuiko.

These times lengthened. Gareth urged her to tell him more about her life in Japan. She delighted in telling him, because he was so interested, attentive.

"As a little girl, I wanted desperately to be Japanese like my friends. I wanted to wear a kimono and zoris and, of course, to celebrate Girls Day like the others."

"Girls Day?"

"Yes, in Japan March third is Girls Day. Sort of a national birthday celebration for girls. There are parties and special gifts for the girl in the family, and she invites her friends to come see the new doll she probably got to add to her collection." Brooke's smile was nostalgic. "My mother was very wise; she allowed me to enjoy Girls Day. As a result I have a wonderful doll collection, as you probably noticed." She pointed with a delicate hand to the china cabinet.

Embarrassed that he had *not* noticed, Gareth glanced at the china cabinet, where in most American homes precious pieces of heirloom china or cut glass were displayed. Now he saw that its shelves were filled with dolls of all sizes, in all sorts of Japanese costumes.

"Oh, my niece would love those!" he commented.

"Your niece?"

"Yes, the Maynards' daughter."

Brooke smiled. "Well, you must bring her by someday to see my dolls."

"Are you sure?" Gareth looked concerned, as if he'd spoken out of turn.

"Of course. I'd be delighted."

"But you're supposed to be recuperating, aren't you? Not having company or entertaining?"

For a moment a shadow seemed to pass over her face, darkening the violet blue eyes for a few seconds. Then Brooke said gently, "I'm not an invalid, Gareth. I like having guests, and I enjoy sharing what I love. My dolls, for instance."

"I'm sorry, I didn't mean to—," Gareth began.

"I know you were just being considerate." Brooke smiled, then added, "You are a very nice man."

As it turned out, Gareth did not bring Cara-Lyn to meet Brooke or see her dolls, after all. Somehow he didn't want to share any of his time with Brooke. He had the feeling that the days of summer were going by fast, speeding in fact, faster than in any summer he had ever known. He was careful not to stay too long on his visits. He was conscious of the watchful presence of Mitsuiko. She was ever alert to the slightest hint of tiredness in Brooke. Then she would immediately but tactfully let it be known that it was time for Gareth to make his departure.

The day came when Gareth took Brooke to Avalon. Brooke looked lovely in a lavender dress, its V-neck ruffled in delicate lace. As she seated herself in the boat, she raised a gaily decorated Japanese paper parasol with a bamboo handle. Before he pulled away from the dock, Gareth impulsively said, "My father would love to paint you."

She smilingly accepted the compliment. Gareth hoped he hadn't embarrassed her with the remark. But it was true. The sun, shadowed by the parasol, gave a special light to her face, an iridescent quality to her dress. They rowed across in silence, hearing only the dipping of the oars, the sound of the water splashing against the side of the boat, a birdsong from somewhere in the top of the trees lining the banks.

When he secured the boat at the dock, he helped her out, then led her up the stone path to the garden. Where the little rise gently sloped down to the lily pond, there was a gracefully shaped bench over which a gentle breeze lifted the drifting fronds of a weeping willow tree.

Brooke drew a long breath. "Oh, Gareth, this is beautiful. It's like a fairyland."

"Actually, it started out as an English country garden. My mother was English—well, no, she was really an American; both my grandparents were Americans, but Mama was born in England. Anyway, she liked the random look of a garden, with flowers and colors all mixed up, no formal beds nor paths, nothing that looked too planned or arranged."

"Japanese gardens are just the opposite," Brooke told him. "They have a beauty all their own. No profusion of colors, variety of flowers. Rocks are more important almost—the arrangement of them is a real art. There is something quite serene. . . . Providing serenity seems to be the underlying purpose of gardens in Japan. And water, the sound of running water, flowing musically over rocks perhaps—it is hard to describe but really soul-refreshing."

"Which do you like best?" Gareth asked, knowing that what he really wanted was for her to express a preference for *his*. Brooke looked at him with tender amusement.

"Do I have to choose?" she asked, laughing lightly. "Rather, ask me what kind of garden I would have for my own if I could."

"All right. Tell me."

"I don't know really. I never imagined having one of my own or thought about what I would like to grow and have my eyes feast upon. When I was in the sanitarium and lying outside, I would daydream about being well, try to place myself in some beautiful, tranquil place—a garden. Of course, having grown up with Japanese gardens, I suppose that's what I envisioned. Japanese gardens are usually small but are created to seem larger, the ends of paths and tiny streams concealed. This gives the impression of hidden space. Symbols are important to Japanese gardeners, and they use them in planning their gardens. Pines, for example, symbolize longevity; the bamboo for strength, the plum tree for delicate beauty, water in small fountains, flowing over rocks into little pools—all combine to express serenity. Japanese gardens tell a secret story not told in bold colors but left to the imagination of the viewer to reflect upon in quietude. In my make-believe garden there were blurred soft colors and meandering paths leading—I don't really know where they led; I never got that far." Brooke halted and laughed softly. "I think I must have drowsed off by then. Still, I remember it made me happy to think about it. A lovely fantasy."

"It doesn't have to be a dream, Brooke. Tell me what you want, and I'll make a garden for you."

Brooke touched his arm gently. "Oh, Gareth, you are reckless! Maybe it is best just to have an inward garden, to contemplate, to wander through, a kind of spiritual place where one can meditate, refresh oneself from everyday realities."

"A *real* garden could be that."

"Maybe," Brooke sighed. Then she gestured to the expanse of rocks, of pinks, lobelia, dahlias, in shades from yellow to pale lavender. "To create a garden like this takes a long time . . ." Her voice trailed away, and for some reason Gareth felt a chill on his heart. It was almost as if Brooke were saying *too long*, as though . . . but he didn't even want to finish the thought.

Gareth sat quietly, watching Brooke. He still thought her the loveliest creature he had ever seen. She had stopped talking and seemed lost in thought.

It was then he knew he loved her and would go on loving her for the rest of his life, no matter what.

Later when he took her inside the house, she exclaimed, "Oh, Gareth, it's just the way I imagined William Morris's Kenscott."

"Maybe that's what my parents intended; it's probably where the idea came from. Morris, Burne-Jones, and the others in that group were my father's inspiration."

"Everything is so beautiful." Brooke glanced around appreciatively, taking in the tapestries, the heavy carved Jacobean furniture, the panels with scenes of festivities and medieval village fairs that Jeff Montrose had painted.

"My parents often quoted William Morris's golden rule for decorating: 'Have nothing in your houses which you do not know to be useful or believe to be beautiful.'"

Brooke turned to smile at Gareth. "That's very much the same philosophy the Japanese have for their homes."

And you fit in perfectly, Gareth thought, gazing at her fondly. Her classic features, the dark hair that waved softly about her face, the slender neck, the flowing ruffles on her pastel dress . . . *Oh, Brooke, my darling, you belong here if ever anyone belonged at Avalon.* Gareth's heart was near to bursting. He longed to sweep Brooke into his arms, kiss her lovely mouth, tell her how much he loved her, longed for her to fill his life, which had been so empty until now. . . .

"I think you'd better take me back now, Gareth," her low voice broke into his thoughts.

Suddenly he felt contrite. There were shadows under her eyes, a look of weariness on her face. It had been too much for her, he thought guiltily. After all, she was recovering from a long illness.

"Of course. We'll leave right now."

She leaned on his arm as they went down the winding path to the dock, so light a weight it might have been a child holding on to him. He carefully put her in the boat, and they rowed across the river to the other bank, where he helped her out. Then as he assisted her up into the passenger seat of the pickup, Gareth belatedly was struck by its inappropriateness. He should have borrowed Lynette's sedan. All the way back on the short ride to Shadowlawn, he chastised himself for his thoughtlessness. Brooke deserved a better vehicle to ride in than this.

As he escorted her up to the porch steps, a worried-looking Mitsuiko came out. Speaking rapidly in Japanese, she came rushing to Brooke's other side and assisted her up the porch steps. She gave Gareth a fierce look. It was the first time the Japanese lady had ever directly looked him in the eyes. *Why, she's angry,* Gareth thought with surprise. Then he realized Mitsuiko was upset because she felt the day had been too much for her friend.

And he was responsible. At the door Brooke turned to Gareth with a wan smile. "Thank you for a beautiful afternoon, Gareth. I enjoyed it very much." Gareth felt dismissed. He also felt concerned and unhappy. He wanted to do something to help. He wanted to get back into Mitsuiko's good graces, to explain he hadn't meant to keep Brooke longer than was good for her. But he didn't have a chance. "Good evening, Gareth," Brooke said and went into the house. Mitsuiko firmly closed the door, leaving him standing on the porch.

The next afternoon he came by with a huge bouquet of mixed flowers. Mitsuiko met him at the door and coolly told him Brooke was resting. She took the flowers and bowed politely and thanked him.

"Please give Miss Leslie my regards," he said. "Tell her I hope she will be feeling better"—the door was already closing—"soon," he finished weakly.

That evening Gareth could not settle down. He was worried and not a little irritated with the high-handed way Mitsuiko had treated him. All the way home Gareth fumed. Had the trip over to Avalon been too much for her? He blamed himself if it had exhausted her.

In the morning he drove back over to Shadowlawn. This time he kept Mitsuiko from shutting the door on him, by opening the screen and planting himself firmly in the frame. "I'm concerned about Miss Leslie, Mitsuiko. I don't know if she has a local doctor, but if she doesn't—"

Just then he heard Brooke's voice calling. Mitsuiko inclined her head, listening intently. A slight frown brought her dark-winged eyebrows over her almond-shaped eyes. Her mouth pursed slightly, then she stepped back, bowed. "Miss Leslie say she would like to see you, Mr. Montrose. She is out on the side porch."

Relieved, Gareth went inside the house and out to where Brooke was reclining on the wicker chaise. She was wearing a kimono and looking well. In fact, he thought she looked blooming. Her cheeks were rosy and her eyes bright. He didn't realize she was running a fever, always a danger sign for one with her condition.

"Mitsuiko is sometimes overprotective," Brooke said, smiling. She took the bouquet Gareth handed her. "I have to remind myself sometimes not to overdo it. Especially when I am having such a good time."

Gareth felt relieved. Everything was all right. "I'm glad. I was afraid I'd worn you out, bored you . . ."

"Bored me?" Brooke laughed her marvelous lilting laugh. "Heavens, no! You'd never do that, Gareth. I loved seeing your garden, your home. It gave me a real window into your childhood and why you grew up to be such"—she hesitated, as if not sure how to say it—"an interesting man." It wasn't exactly what she had intended to say, but she had not wanted to embarrass him by using words like "sensitive" or "poetic." American men took great pride in being thought masculine.

However, Gareth felt a warmth sweep all through him. The fact that Brooke understood and appreciated even the things he left unspoken made him happy and grateful. *I love you, Brooke Leslie, don't you know that? Dare I tell you?*

"Thank you again for your thoughtfulness," Brooke said.

She was tactful but he also felt he wasn't to stay longer. At least not today.

He got back into his pickup. But he felt too elated, too full of excess energy, to go back to Avalon, to be alone. He had to tell someone, talk about Brooke to someone. Not reveal everything he was feeling but just talk about her. He'd go see Lynette.

chapter

9

WASHINGTON, D.C., was beastly hot in June, and Richmond was worse. Lynette Maynard fanned herself. It was delicious to be home at Spring Hill, with nearly two months of relaxation ahead before Frank had to start campaigning again. She leaned her head back against the chintz pillows on the white wicker rocker on her screened-in porch. She fully intended to enjoy every minute of her vacation from the social whirl of being a state senator's wife. Cara-Lyn was working as a camp counselor in the mountains, and Lynette and Frank could look forward to a blissful, quiet time together, far away from politics, the press. She closed her eyes and sighed. How restful it was here.

Her respite was short-lived. A few minutes later the roar of a motor coming up the drive startled her. She sat up just in time to see her brother's pickup pull to a stop, scattering the gravel stones in front of the house. He jumped out of the cab of his truck, waved.

She put down her fan, got up, and walked to the edge of the porch. "Gareth! What on earth! . . . What brings you out here in the middle of the day? Nothing wrong, I hope?"

"Nothing's wrong, Sis. In fact, everything's pretty near perfect."

Lynette frowned. "Well, come on up and tell me all about it!"

An hour later she watched his truck disappear down the drive. She sat back in her chair and rocked steadily for a few minutes. Who would ever have dreamed it? Of all the attractive, eligible young ladies she had trotted out on various occasions, hoping one of them would catch her elusive bachelor brother's eye, he had gone and fallen in love with someone behind her back. And someone totally unsuitable, at that. Well, maybe not *unsuitable* exactly, but someone so unexpected. A missionary—isn't that what the realtor had told them? Or maybe Frank hadn't got it straight. Whatever, something was lost in the translation. She had assumed that a middle-aged *male* missionary recovering from a serious illness was to rent the Maynard house for six months. Certainly not the beauty of intelligence and charm Gareth had described.

Well, there was nothing to do but go and see for herself. After all the years she had spent worrying about her brother, his reclusiveness, his solitary lifestyle, he had fallen completely head over heels in love with someone she didn't know. Of course, that could be taken care of right away. She would send a note to Miss Brooke Leslie and ask if she might call. She was sure Gareth had exaggerated. People in love always did. She would find out for herself if Brooke Leslie was the paragon of beauty and virtue he had rhapsodized about.

Lynette drove over to Arbordale in her own small green coupe. Dressed in a beige pongee ensemble, a silk straw hat, bone pumps, and matching gloves and handbag, she was the epitome of a Southern lady making a courtesy call. Of course, it was much more than that.

The bonds between all the children of Jeff and Faith Montrose were unusually close. Lynette not only loved her brother dearly but felt protective and proprietary toward him.

If he was to be in love and marry, it had to be to the right person. Because of their rootless, motherless childhood, Lynette felt Gareth needed someone who would make a *real* home for him. Someone who would support, encourage, and love him unconditionally. Who was this Brooke Leslie? she asked herself. What was she like to have so quickly and completely captured Gareth's heretofore elusive heart?

Well, she'd soon find out, she reminded herself, as she braked her small car in front of the porticoed porch.

A young Japanese woman in a kimono patterned in indigo blue and gray opened the door to her, took the calling card Lynette handed her, then shyly ushered her into the living room.

Lynette stood in the center of the room and slowly pivoted. Her tenant had changed things a great deal, she noted. The last time Lynette was here, the house had been cluttered with overstuffed furniture, heavy draperies, framed dark landscapes. Now it looked serene and spare. Slatted bamboo curtains now hung at the windows, letting in light; striped cotton slipcovers concealed the ornate tapestries of sofa, armchairs. Artistic flower arrangements replaced the clutter of knickknacks favored in the Victorian era, when the house had first been decorated.

Lynette's eyes were drawn to the mantelpiece, on which were displayed a collection of strange little figures. She walked over to examine them. Less than two inches high, they were superbly carved of ivory or some rare wood. There was a small turtle, several funny little men doing various kinds of work, a basket of fish, and a tiny rabbit gazing up with a whimsical expression. As Lynette leaned forward to take a closer look, a soft voice behind her spoke.

"You're admiring my Netsuke collection."

Lynette turned to see a tall, willowy brunette standing in the arched doorway.

"Yes. I've never seen anything like them. They're delightful."

"Thank you. And welcome. I'm Brooke Leslie, and you of course are Gareth's sister. I would know that anywhere. There's a strong family resemblance. I suppose everyone tells you that."

"Yes, we do look alike, except for our younger sister, Bryanne, who is blond."

"Do sit down." Brooke gestured to one of the armchairs. "Will you have tea?"

"That would be nice. I must apologize for not calling upon you sooner. My husband was kept at the state capitol longer than usual—several pending bills—and we just arrived home last week. Actually, I've just been catching my breath, being lazy."

As if on cue, Mitsuiko came in, bearing a tray with tea things. Lynette noticed the small decorated teapot, the handle-less cups, of Japanese porcelain. When Brooke introduced Mitsuiko as her companion, Lynette was a little taken aback. She had assumed she was the maid.

"Mitsuiko's father is a professor at the university. Her family kindly allowed her to accompany me to the States," Brooke explained.

While Brooke poured their tea, Lynette observed her hostess. Brooke Leslie *was* beautiful, as Gareth had said. However, Lynette saw things a man like Gareth would not notice. She saw fine lines around her eyes and around her mouth. Whether these were caused from her illness or possibly her age, Lynette was not sure. Were those a few threads of silver in the massed dark hair? These too could be brought on prematurely by a long illness. Lynette felt she must be at least a few years older than her brother. Gareth was thirty-two. Brooke Leslie must be at least thirty-five or thirty-six.

Her age and fragile health could be a problem. Lynette had always hoped her brother would marry, have children, carry on their branch of the Montrose family.

The visit was like a deep pond—it was smooth and pleasant on the surface, but underneath, in the consciousness of both women, swirled many conflicting thoughts. There were subjects that needed to be explained or discussed but which, both of them knew, would never be.

Before she rose to leave, Lynette asked, "Is there anything I can do for you? Any shopping you need done? I mean, it must be difficult for Mitsuiko to deal with things in a strange town, in another language."

"That is very kind of you to suggest, thank you, but Mitsuiko actually does quite well. English is a second language taught in Japanese schools."

"I just thought"—Lynette gathered her gloves and handbag—"there might be something . . ."

As they walked to the front door, Brooke said, "As a matter of fact, perhaps there is something—that is, if it wouldn't be too much trouble. A book at the library? Mitsuiko has gone there, but I'm afraid her selection . . ." Brooke laughed. "Her taste runs to stories about orphans. In fact, her favorite book is *Anne of Green Gables*. She adores *'Anne of the Red Hair,'* as she calls it. Red hair being a rarity in Japan, it is probably part of the appeal."

"Of course. I'd be delighted," Lynette answered. "I'm afraid I'm not up on the latest books; I don't seem to have a great deal of time to read. What sort of book do you like? Novels?"

"I really enjoy travel books. Maybe because I haven't had the opportunity to do so very much. One about Italy?"

At the door they said good-bye.

Brooke stood there watching as Lynette's car went down the driveway and disappeared at the end, where the hedge hid the road. What impression had Gareth's sister taken away with her? she wondered. How did it match what Gareth had probably told her?

Lynette made the turn onto the road back to Mayfield thoughtfully. Brooke Leslie was lovely but almost as though enclosed in glass. You could see through it enough to see a woman physically beautiful but untouched and untouchable. Her refinement was obvious. Her manners were faultless. What lay behind that gracious smile, those thoughtful eyes? Lynette hoped her brother was not on the brink of heartbreak.

chapter
10

ONE AFTERNOON GARETH came by Shadowlawn with flowers, fruit. As he was leaving, Brooke said, "Mitsuiko reminded me I have been remiss."

"What do you mean?"

"You have been so kind to us—"

"My pleasure entirely," Gareth interrupted.

Brooke smiled. "Let me finish. She said I should have returned your graciousness, invited you to dinner some evening." She tilted her head to one side questioningly. "Would you like to sample Japanese cooking? I believe that is Mitsuiko's main purpose; she would like to show off her culinary skill."

"Why, yes, I would. Very much. Thank you."

"You must realize this will be Mitsuiko's treat. I confess I cannot boil the proverbial egg. I'm quite hopeless in the kitchen. It's not something I'm proud of, it's just the truth," she added. "I thought you should know that."

"In the interest of truth between friends, right?" Gareth grinned.

"Exactly," she said, smiling. "Then shall we say next Thursday?"

That evening Gareth arrived to find Brooke dressed in a Japanese kimono of lustrous, cream-colored silk. The obi, a wide sash circling the waist, was a deep coral shade. Her hair was twisted up from her neck and secured with two long teak hair sticks.

"Mitsuiko insisted I play hostess in traditional dress."

"I'm glad she did. You look"—Gareth faltered, wondering how to tell her how beautiful and exotic he thought she looked—"quite lovely."

Mitsuiko had placed a low table and two pillows out on the screened-in porch. Flickering candles in glass holders set on the screen ledge cast a soft glow. As they seated themselves on opposite sides of the table, Mitsuiko began bringing in the various dishes one at a time in her quiet, smiling manner. Everything was presented arranged artistically on separate plates. Nothing was heaped on plates, as Gareth had seen bountiful Southern dinners served. Each course was almost a sample of the wide variety of Japanese delicacies—thinly sliced carrots, cucumbers, a clear soup, a main dish of tiny shrimp, mushrooms, vegetables, a narrow piece of white fish, individual bowls of rice. Cups of soy sauce were placed at the left of each place for dipping.

Although everything tasted strange and new to Gareth, he tried it all, aware that Mitsuiko was watching anxiously, and not unaware of the amusement in Brooke's eyes. When the tea was brought at the end of the meal, Gareth praised Mitsuiko heartily. She murmured her thanks, ducking her head shyly. It was obvious she was enormously pleased that her dinner had been such a success.

"You must let me return your hospitality," Gareth said as he prepared to leave shortly after they finished. "Not that I could match anything like this. But my sister Lynette has suggested several times that I bring you out to her house, Spring Hill."

A shadow passed over Brooke's face, and she said, "I hope you understand, Gareth, but I'm not going out socially just yet."

"Of course," he said quickly. "I am just passing on Lynette's invitation. I didn't mean to pressure you."

"I know, and I do appreciate both the thought and your understanding."

He looked as if he were about to say more, thought better of it. Soon, thinking she looked a little tired, he said good night and left. Standing in the doorway, Brooke followed the taillights on his truck until it went around the bend in the driveway and disappeared.

Her sense of uneasiness about Gareth's more and more evident feelings for her sharpened. She could not deny any longer that their relationship had gone beyond friendship. She hadn't meant for this to happen, had never dreamed of such a thing. Long ago she had decided that kind of love was out of the question for her.

It was her fault, she thought, sighing. She had been lonely for so long. Then unexpectedly Gareth had come into her life. Maybe she should have stopped it before it reached this point. But she had so enjoyed his company. They had so many mutual interests—gardens, flowers, music, art. His warmth, spontaneity, was so different from some of the men she had known in a limited way before. Certainly from the Japanese men, who were so careful, reticent, secretive. Gareth was a direct contrast. He was *so* American, so warm, generous, open.

He had been eager to share his thoughts, talk about his feelings. In his own words, truth and trust were the main ingredients of any relationship. If they didn't exist, nothing lasting or worthwhile could happen between two people. Remembering when he had said that, Brooke felt stricken. Truth, at least not the complete truth as far as she was concerned, had not yet been revealed. Would it be necessary?

Even as she pondered and worried a little about this, Brooke had not expected to have to face it so soon.

August came, the end of summer, with the last profusion of flowers and fruit from Avalon. Gareth came more and more often, bringing the abundance of his labor. They had known each other a little over four months.

Then one evening when they were sitting together in the lovely lavender dusk on the porch at Shadowlawn, he could no longer keep what he was feeling to himself. Before she could stop him, he had poured out his heart.

"I've known almost from the first that I love you, Brooke. I didn't want to tell you. I was afraid I'd frighten you, that you would think I was too impetuous, too shallow . . . but I am so sure of what I feel, I had to say it. I love you." He reached for her hand, brought it to his lips and kissed it.

"Oh, Gareth, I'm touched—flattered really—that you should feel this way about me. But there is so much you don't know—things that if you did know, would make you realize that what you think you want can never be."

"Why do you say that?" he demanded. "I know all I want to know, all I need to know. I love you. Isn't that all that matters?"

"We've only known each other this summer."

"Does length of time really make that much difference? We've spent hours together, talked . . . Some people go their whole lives long and never know what we have shared in these few months."

"Yes, but—" Brooke hesitated, then said, "Listen, Gareth, there are things you should know about me. Things I haven't told you. Then maybe you'll understand. If I tell you a little about . . . my circumstances." Gently she pulled her hand away, and reluctantly he released it. Then he leaned forward, ready to listen.

"I planned to become a missionary. Like my parents, whom I admired very much. I entered nurses' training. It was—rather it proved—too rigorous for me. My health broke and I had to—" She paused. "My parents were told I might die."

Gareth started to say something, but she put a finger on his mouth, shook her head. "Please, let me finish. I was sent to a sanitarium in the mountains, much like the Alps—snow-covered, air very clear and cold. We patients were bundled up and placed outside on lounge chairs. It was supposed to be very healing, invigorating. It was there God told me, 'No.'" Her smile was sad. "Yes, God sometimes speaks even to someone like me. It was almost audible. I was lying out in my cot, desperate and sick, praying. I wanted to be well so I could get back to my training. And then it became very clear that was not God's will for my life, that I would have to find some other way to serve him."

Gareth reached for her hand again, but Brooke tucked it into the sleeve of her kimono and continued. "Months went by and I made better progress than the doctors had anticipated. However, they were very honest with me. I would never completely regain my health. I would always have to be careful; there would always be the possibility of a relapse. I couldn't expect to live a normal life, the kind of life most women hope to have—marriage, children. That's why you must not think of that kind of love with me, Gareth. It cannot be."

"I don't accept that," Gareth said firmly. "Love is miraculous. Love has healing powers of its own. I love you, Brooke. More than anything in the world, I want us to be married. I want to take care of you. I want to make you happy, to protect you. I don't expect anything of you. I just want us to be together. That's all."

"But Gareth," Brooke gently protested, "you don't know what that might involve. My health is unstable—I'm fine now, better, much better than when I came, but you can never really say—and I'm older than you, Gareth, by quite a few years,

I imagine. I could never be a real wife, give you what you deserve—a real home, children . . ."

"None of that would matter if I had you," he protested. "Don't you see that, Brooke? Can't you tell how much I love you?"

She shook her head sorrowfully. "Gareth, you're so dear and impulsive, and I love you for it. I understand what you're saying, and I know you mean it now . . . but have you ever heard the quotation 'The longing of the moment seems the essential; one is apt to forget the eternity of regret'? It would break my heart, Gareth, if years from now—or even a year from now—you would regret your reckless proposal."

"No, I wouldn't. Never," he declared vehemently. "This summer has been like something out of a dream—a dream I've had all my life, I think. One I never thought would come true."

Brooke drew out her hand, and her fingers touched his chin. She looked deeply into his eyes and said, "The Japanese believe in fate, Gareth, and timing. If we had met earlier—perhaps. Too much of my life has gone by. For years I've lived as if I were an invalid. Such a different life than yours, and—"

"It doesn't matter about the past, the disappointments, the dreams that didn't come true—yours or mine. You're here now and I'm here, and by some marvelous coincidence we met. Maybe that's why you didn't become a missionary. God works in mysterious ways, doesn't he? Maybe being a missionary was your idea, not his. Maybe we were supposed to meet, be together."

Brooke smiled indulgently. She knew there was no use trying to persuade Gareth to accept what she felt was the truth, the impossibility of their future. But there was a wistfulness in her eyes as she looked at him, his broad shoulders, his vitality, his youthful strength. She kept silent, however, recalling the

Japanese quotation "Happiness is like a butterfly, lightly resting then flying off, not to be held or grasped," and tried to keep the moment. For now it was enough that this wonderful young man, with all his vigor, enthusiasm, loved her . . . for this moment. After all, that was all anyone could be sure of . . . this single moment in time.

chapter
11

ONCE GARETH HAD DECLARED his love, he traveled on the high road of optimism. He had total confidence that whatever obstacles stood in the way of complete fulfillment of his dream would be removed in time. His few moments of uncertainty were infrequent. When they came, it was from, of all places, an unexpected source.

He had heard the description "inscrutable Oriental," but as he met Mitsuiko's gaze, he had the firm conviction that she knew something. Not only about his feelings for Brooke but about something else. What? He couldn't tell. There was something in her eyes—understanding, sympathy? Whatever it was quickly vanished when he looked at her, trying to find it out. She would quickly lower her eyes, making it impossible for him to read anything in them.

After that evening they never discussed the future again. Gareth believed his love was strong enough to overcome Brooke's arguments. He would prove to her that his conviction was able to surmount any difficulties she could put forth. It would just take a little more time to convince her.

Little did he know he was living in a fool's paradise while

Brooke, facing the reality, was making her own plans. Time was running out.

Both of them dwelled in a subtle fantasy of never-ending time. Fragile as the fluttering butterflies among the flowers were those hours of unspoiled happiness they spent in the garden. Yet there was always the shadow of those events happening in other parts of the world. One could not completely erase the screaming headlines, the horror of what was going on in England, where the Montrose family had ties.

It was, in all respects, a bittersweet summer, a summer that came too swiftly to an end. It was time for Brooke to leave, for her and Mitsuiko to return to Japan.

On an early September day, golden with sunlight, the maple leaves just beginning to display their vivid autumn colors, Brooke knew she could delay no longer. For a week she had known but had not been able to bring herself to break the news to Gareth. Her tickets had arrived from the steamship line, her train reservations to the West Coast were confirmed, and all that was left was to tell Gareth.

It was a beautiful evening, clear and cool and full of stars, as Gareth drove to Arbordale. His heart throbbed with anticipation, longing for the evening ahead with her. In his corduroy jacket pocket was the little blue enameled brooch, set with tiny Australian crystals, he had found almost by chance. Actually, he had been searching for some sort of beautiful ring to give her as an engagement ring. He had been looking in the window of the small jewelry store in Mayfield that specialized in antique and estate jewelry and individual designs, when he spotted it. It was about one inch across. In the shape of a tiny turtle, it had reminded him of the one in her Netsuke collection. He had gone in and bought it, knowing it was just the sort of whimsical thing she would love.

As Brooke waited for Gareth to come, all the many impressions, incidents, times spent together, merged in her thoughts. It had been an idyllic summer, far more special than she had ever imagined it would be. She had planned a summer of rest, relaxation, tranquillity. She had not dreamed of love.

Brooke recalled the first time she had met Gareth Montrose. He had the air of a man equally at home in a cabin or castle. His physical presence was intense — tall, well-built, his skin healthily tanned, his hair thick, dark, wavy, his eyes clear, truthseeking. She had felt almost overwhelmed by his strength and vitality. Now that she had come to know him, she realized he had another kind of strength, a spiritual one that was even more powerful. Gareth was pure, in a way few men are. It shone from his intensely blue eyes, it spoke in his every sentence, his every action. He was generous, kind, intelligent, unselfish. In another lifetime he would have been one of the idealistic band of King Arthur's Round Table. She smiled at her own analogy, knowing Gareth would be embarrassed and scoff at such a description.

She knew she had to tell him she was leaving, and the thought of doing so left her cold and a little shaky. It was even harder than she had anticipated.

Gareth reacted first with shock, then disbelief, then anger.

"But you knew I would have to . . . someday," she protested gently.

"But not this soon. Not now. Not when you know I love you."

He paced the room with long strides for a few minutes, then whirled around, came over, knelt down beside her chair, took both her thin hands in his, brought them to his lips, kissed them.

"I don't want you to go. I can't bear to think of your going."

"I have to go, don't you see that? I promised Mitsuiko's family I would take her back with me within the year. I can't break my promise." She paused, then asked softly, "You wouldn't want me to, really, would you, Gareth? A promise is a promise. Honor is everything in Japan. To break your word is about the worst thing you can do."

Gareth, brought up as he had been with the ancient code of chivalry and the honor imbued in every Southern gentleman, shook his head slowly. He searched her face lingeringly, then said in a very low voice, "I wish I could make time stand still. Just as it is. Now. I don't want anything ever to change."

"But Gareth, don't you realize nothing stays the same, not ever? The world is spinning constantly, and we're each of us changing minute by minute. That's what makes life—change. That's what makes it so interesting and exciting."

"No!" he said vehemently. "I've just found you, Brooke. Never before in my life have I been so sure of anything as I am that we were meant for each other." He held up his hand to ward off any protests she might be readying. "You must marry me. We'll get a place in the mountains. Higher elevation, better for your health. I'll build the cabin myself. It will be rustic but will have all the amenities . . . and a good road so that if you need to be checked regularly by a doctor, that can be managed. The pure mountain air will equal what you told me about that place in Japan. Oh, darling Brooke, we'll be so happy. Please just say yes. I love you and I promise to cherish, protect, and care for you all the days of my life. I can't let you go. I *won't* let you go."

He was on his knees now beside her chair. His arms circled her waist and he looked up at her.

Brooke's resistance broke. She was being offered the pearl of great value, the one thing she thought was lost to her forever. The devotion, the love, of a man. And such a man. Maybe this was God's gift to her. She would be ungrateful not to accept it.

"Oh, Gareth, dearest—" Her voice trembled. "If you really think . . . if you really want . . ."

"I do! Say, yes, Brooke, say yes!"

They talked for another hour, an hour happily mingled with long, tender looks, soft words, gentle kisses. Brooke explained she had to go ahead with her plans now but would return and then, God willing, they would be married. In the meantime Gareth would look for mountain property, start designing their rustic retreat.

"How long will you be gone?" he asked, as if the words hurt him physically to say.

"A few months at the most. I'll have to close up my little house, say good-bye to friends." She smiled. "You know, the usual things—packing up belongings, books, and so on I left behind."

He looked so miserable, she touched his cheek with her palm, stroking it lightly. "Gareth, dear, it won't be long. The time will pass before you know it."

She tried to make the tone of her voice optimistic. She had to ignore the dark premonition lurking in her heart. She knew she must keep her own fears, her foreboding, to herself, not let it spill over and somehow darken his bright hope.

Gareth, my love, remember that I love you, that we love each other. No matter what the future holds, this time we've had together will always be one of my most cherished memories—

As if he had read her mind, Gareth burst out, "Please let me come with you. I could help you tie up loose ends, do whatever needs to be done. That way it would go faster. We could come back together—"

She shook her head. "No, that would be impossible. In Japan things are not done that way. Americans are always in a rush; they want to get things done, finished, as quickly as they efficiently can. In Japan there is protocol, the formal way of doing things with courtesy, tradition."

"I can hardly stand to think of your leaving. I never wanted this summer to end. I wanted us to go on and on. I love you and will love you for two thousand years. Forever." He looked at her with great intensity. Her gaze met his and held and lingered as if they were looking into each other's souls.

After a lingering good-bye, he left and went down the path, through the gate, in a haze of anguish.

When the sound of Gareth's truck faded and finally could not be heard, Brooke turned from the front door. She felt suddenly exhausted. The emotion of their parting had wrung her. She went to the staircase and stood there, holding on to the newel post before starting up to her bedroom.

As she took the first step, her legs trembled. She clung to the railing for support, wondering if she could make it up the stairway. Her heart beat rapidly. "Mitsuiko!" she called weakly. She felt the choking cough come. "Mitsuiko!"

At Avalon, Gareth tossed restlessly. He told himself things always seemed worse at night. In the morning everything would seem better. Things would work out. In the sunlight— when corners were not filled with shadows, and the gloom was not seeping in like fog into the room, wrapping itself around his heart and mind, dragging him down—everything would regain its normal perspective, its ordinary size, not loom over him like monstrous giants of despair.

The day Brooke was due to leave for Richmond to take the train to San Francisco, she woke unrested from a dream-ridden sleep. She felt she had spent a sleepless night. It was gray dark when she woke up, the furniture hardly discernible in the dimness of the room. Her heart was heavy.

Yet during this long night—mystics sometimes call it the dark night of the soul—Brooke had begun to see that it was not a question of courage, was not that she felt she could not relinquish her responsibility to Mitsuiko's family. It was what Gareth asked, what he deserved, what her love for him longed to give. She could have made the commitment in good faith in happier days, but now there was always the dark possibility hanging over them that she might not live to return and fulfill her promise to marry him.

She had not told Gareth about her bad spell. Mitsuiko, alarmed at her call, had come running from her bedroom to help Brooke up to bed. Brooke protested that a day's rest would revive her. But there had been too much emotional strain. The idea of their approaching departure had been taxing. It was the very thing the doctors had warned her about. She called Gareth the next afternoon, disguising her weariness. Giving the excuse that she and Mitsuiko had many things to attend to, she told Gareth that it would be better for him not to come for a day or so. He offered help but finally accepted her word.

In those few days when she did not see Gareth, an inner knowing grew within Brooke that was more than intuition. She felt bereft. She tried to shake it but it would not go away. It was something she couldn't define. A shadow hovering on them, threatening their future happiness.

On the day of their departure, Gareth, already fighting sadness and depression, drove Brooke and Mitsuiko to the train station. Brooke sat in the front beside him, and he held her hand most of the way, except when he had to shift gears. Mitsuiko, in the back, which was piled high with their luggage, smiled happily. Why not? She was going home. It would be a long trip, but at the end of their journey she would be welcomed by parents, family, friends. She was going to something she knew and loved, not leaving anything behind.

At the station there was much to be done to get them settled in their compartment. He helped them stow their luggage, demonstrated to Mitsuiko how the little table between the windows came up, and opened the door to show her the tiny washroom. She smiled, bowed, shiny almond eyes sparkling. Then they heard the conductor coming through the train, down the aisle. It was time at last to say good-bye, for Gareth to get off and watch the train pull out, taking his beloved with it.

"You will telegraph as soon as you get to San Francisco, let me know how the trip was, won't you?" he said, and his voice sounded unnaturally stern. "Or phone long distance from the hotel. I'll wait for your call."

Brooke protested. "Oh, Gareth, I don't know. There's a time difference, you see, and—"

"I want to hear your voice, Brooke," he said, and his own broke a little.

"All right," she said in a hoarse whisper. "Yes, I will."

They looked at each other for a long time—an eternity, it seemed—each memorizing the face of the one they loved.

"You'd better go, Gareth," Brooke said at last.

"I know." He took her slowly into his arms. Her head rested on his shoulder, and she closed her eyes, feeling for one last time the strength of his embrace as his arms tightened around her slender waist.

"God keep you, darling," she said.

He found it impossible to speak. She turned her head and their lips met in a kiss.

In that kiss was everything they felt for each other. But mingled with it was the heartbreak of inevitable farewell.

They heard the conductor's last call coming from outside. "All aboard!"

"You must go, Gareth, love." Brook drew back from his embrace. "Good-bye."

"Take care of her, Mitsuiko," he flung over his shoulder as he left the compartment, rushed down the aisle, not looking back. He swung down from the car and stood on the platform until the train started rolling along the track. Then he began running alongside as it moved forward, gaining speed. Brooke pressed her cheek against the window, keeping his tall figure in sight as long as possible. Then with a deep sigh she fell back against the upholstered seat, shut her eyes, two tears rolling down her pale face.

It must be some form of masochism, Gareth told himself roughly as he swerved his pickup into the driveway of Shadowlawn. Already the yard and garden showed signs of neglect. He needed to check with Lynette, find out what she and Frank planned to do with the house over the winter. He got out of the cab, slammed the door, and went around to the side of the house where he and Brooke had spent so many languorously happy hours together.

He felt her presence strongly, as if she were about to enter the garden, come through the trellis, look up from her book with a smile—Brooke, Brooke! Her name was like a sharp stone in his chest. He missed her so much. He longed to see her, to kiss the gentle mouth, smooth back the fine silky hair from the pale brow, the shadows of her long lashes on her cheeks . . .

For a minute he stood very still and let the sense of her presence come over him. It was almost as real, as tangible, as her absence. But it was gone almost before he could grasp it. . . . He certainly could not hold on to it. He was reminded of the haiku she once read to him out of a slim book of Japanese poetry: "Happiness is like a butterfly, impossible to capture; all one can do is hope it will alight on your shoulder for a brief moment."

Gareth clung to every memory they had shared. Holding on to them made Brooke seem closer. But even as he willed it, the reality of it slipped away. Each empty day, each day without her, made the memory of those months dimmer. Her letters were few and far between. He read them line for line, hoping, praying, for some definite word of her plans to return. Weeks went by, slipping into months, and then . . .

Lynette, in her dressing gown, was at the breakfast table, eating a leisurely morning meal. She picked up the newspaper still folded at her plate. Then she saw the headlines: "Japanese Intern All Foreigners, American Nationals." She gasped. She wondered if Gareth knew. She didn't think her brother even took a daily newspaper. He did get the *Messenger* that was delivered once a week, when he went into Arbordale to pick up his mail, but sometimes she didn't think he even bothered to read it. She put the paper down and went into the hall, picked up the phone. With stiff fingers she started to dial Gareth's number.

Then she replaced the phone. No, that would be too big a shock if he hadn't seen the paper. She would have to go over there, tell him herself. She turned and rushed up the stairs to get dressed.

She ignored speed limits as she drove over to Arbordale, her hands clenching the steering wheel of her little car, her mind already rehearsing how she would break the news to Gareth if he hadn't heard. Oh, dear God, this was tragic. Lynette had always thought his romance with the lovely Brooke Leslie had been doomed from the beginning, for a number of reasons. But this was so unexpected.

At the landing she did not wait to be ferried across to the island but instead hired a small boat and rowed across to Avalon on her own.

She hurried up from the dock and found Gareth in the gardening shed. He looked startled at her sudden appearance, and his cheerful greeting died on his lips with one look at her face.

"What is it, Sis? What's happened?"

Wordlessly she showed him the headlines.

Gareth turned ashen. He took the paper she handed him and scanned the lead article, then dropped it, sank down on the wooden bench, and put his head in his hands. "Dear God," he moaned.

Lynette stood there helplessly. Her heart was breaking for her brother. She made a tentative move toward him. But how could she comfort him? What could she say that would help?

Finally he raised his head and looked at her with haunted eyes. "Internment. Do you know what that can mean? I've read what the Japanese do to their prisoners. The atrocities they committed on the Chinese they captured . . ."

"But these are civilians, Gareth, not soldiers. There are international laws about the treatment of civilians, and we're not at war with the Japanese."

"We may well be soon, if things keep going as they are. Brooke told me there was a strong military presence in Japan that constantly talked about expansion, about how they needed more land . . ." He ran his fingers through his thick, dark hair. "I'm so worried. The conditions in those internment camps can't be anything but horrible. Brooke's health . . ." He lifted his head and looked at his sister with tortured eyes. "My God, Lynette, she could die there."

Deeply moved by his emotion, Lynette reached to take his hand, searching for something, anything, to say but knowing all she could offer was to listen tenderly and sympathetically and let him pour out his heart.

chapter

12

Montclair
December 7, 1941

CARA HAD SPENT THE DAY ALONE. Kip was at the airfield, and
the house seemed so empty without the old sounds of voices
echoing, feet running upon the stairs, dogs barking. She even
missed the pile of muddy boots in the front hall, the dogs
romping in when they were allowed. She missed Niki more
than she told anyone, more than she had imagined possible.
And Luc was in flight training in Texas.

Reports from England of the night air raids by the Nazi
Luftwaffe, which was kept at bay only by the small, brave British
air force, were frightening. How long could they hold out? Cara
was afraid of what Luc might do once he got his wings. Might
he follow his father's example? In the last war against Germany
Kip had joined the Lafayette Esquadrille, the group of
American flyers who had volunteered to fight for France. Ever
since Luc had returned from France after the summer of 1939,
he had talked of joining the Canadian Royal Air Force in order
to help the Allies. He had had a renewed sense of his own link
to France. Luc's French mother, Etienette, had been an ambulance driver in the last war, as had Cara herself.

Cara shuddered, pushing away some of her horrible memories

of that time. Do something, she ordered herself firmly. Keeping busy was the best way to fight the loneliness that threatened to overcome her. She decided to start a job she had put off for months—years, even. That was getting the family's photograph album in order.

At one time Niki had become an avid "shutterbug," after being given a small camera for Christmas. Soon, as happened with many of Niki's enthusiasms, the novelty had worn off, and she had gone on to some other hobby. Cara was then designated to become the chronicler of the events of their lives. Now she got out the large leather album choked with dozens of assorted photos. She sat down at the table in what had formerly been called the library at Montclair but through the chaotic years of their haphazard life had been humorously dubbed the "multipurpose room."

As Cara sorted through the pictures—some still in their original envelope from the developers, others thrust in a hodgepodge of bunches between the covers—she discovered that it was not the chore she had anticipated. Rather, she was enjoying it. Looking at the snapshots of Niki and Luc as little children brought back so many happy memories of the years they were becoming a real family. Luc in the cowboy outfit he'd asked for and received for Christmas. Niki, looking adorable at six, dressed for Easter Sunday in a smocked dress and flowered hat. Luc in his VMI uniform, and another of him at the Mayfield horse show, standing beside his horse and proudly holding his trophy. Niki with her beloved Shetland pony, Sugar, then later with her horse, Maggie. Still another of her, in sharp contrast, looking demure in her white graduation dress, carrying a bouquet of roses tied with a satin ribbon on which was written "Class of 1939." That was in June, right before she left for what was to be a summer in France.

There were many of Kip. Cara noticed this with some

amusement, because they had usually been taken by her when she was trying to finish a roll of film. Kip with both children at various ages, on horseback or behind the wheel of the vintage roadster that he refused to sell or trade in for a more modern car. He periodically polished it, even though he no longer drove it. Cara studied her husband's face, thinking how little he had actually changed. Of course, there was some gray at his temples, but that only made him look distinguished. He was still as handsome as he'd been in his twenties. She came across one she had not taken. Somehow this had got slipped in among the more recent ones. It was of Kip in front of his plane, looking confident and with that slightly amused expression, as if he found the world continually surprising. Where had this been snapped? Cara squinted, looking closer. At an airfield in France? And by whom? Kitty? Her twin had once been engaged to Kip. Or was it the French girl he had fallen in love with who became Luc's mother?

Cara was totally absorbed in what she was doing, and the afternoon passed almost unnoticed. When she heard the sound of tires on the gravel driveway, she looked up at the mantel clock and was astonished to see it was nearly five o'clock. Kip was home! Outside, the winter day was darkening. She heard his footsteps on the porch, the front door opening and slamming shut behind him. Then he was standing in the arched entrance to the library.

One look at his face and immediately Cara knew that something was dreadfully wrong. She felt a cold fist of dread in the pit of her stomach. Had something happened to one of the children? To Luc? Or Niki? She started to get up, and all the loose snapshots spilled from the album she had on her lap.

"Haven't you had the radio on?" Kip demanded.

"No, I've been—" She stopped abruptly. "Why?"

"The Japanese have bombed Pearl Harbor. It means war."

1942

chapter
13

AFTER DECEMBER SEVENTH, Gareth could no longer put aside the wrenching conflicts of his conscience. Boyhood friends were joining up before they got drafted, making choices as to which branch of the service they wanted to join. He could no longer avoid the issue, no longer equivocate, no longer study how he could put his knowledge of horticulture, landscaping, to a creditable war use. Still, his lifelong horror of war persisted, influenced no doubt by the attitude of his father, Jeff, and the pacifism of Kitty Traherne. He finally convinced himself that if he tried to enlist in some kind of alternative service, it might be construed as "draft dodging" and bring down the scorn and wrath of relatives like Stewart and Luc, who had already joined, respectively, the navy and air force. He could no longer sit on the fence; he had to act.

War propaganda was at a fever pitch, enlistments were high, the patriotism of all was up for scrutiny and examination. When Gareth decided to report to the draft board and declare himself a conscientious objector, he knew he would be exposing his deep-felt convictions to the scathing skepticism of some. Knowing he could not shield himself, Gareth hung on to his resolve.

Outwardly composed, he felt keenly the steely-eyed contempt of some of the members of the draft board, the tinge of sarcasm in the voice of the chairman as he was questioned. With only slightly concealed disgust, the man ordered Gareth to fill out additional papers, then wait to be assigned.

Gareth had known it would not be easy, but he had not realized it would be this hard. He felt as visible as Jews in Nazi Germany must have felt with the yellow stars sewn prominently on their coat sleeves.

However, it was a choice he had made without anyone's counsel, approval, or disapproval. He knew he had laid himself wide open to criticism, not only from those of the public who knew of his decision but also from members of his own family. He was made aware of relatives who disagreed violently with his stand.

Aunt Kitty was the only one who understood. She had written him a beautiful letter, which he kept folded in the inside pocket of his jacket so he could take it out every so often and reread it. In it she wrote,

> *Sometimes courage is construed as cowardice. That is when we must be strong and show by our actions that this label is wrong. I believe this quote from J. F. Clarke says it all: "Conscience is the root of all true courage; if a man would be brave, let him obey his conscience." I know you are a good man, honest, true to your convictions, and I pray God's blessing on you wherever this leads you.*

Where it led Gareth was to a janitorial job in an army hospital on the West Coast.

The dirtiest, grubbiest, most menial tasks were allotted to him, along with the mocking sneers of the sergeant in charge, who issued orders, assigned duties.

However, when Gareth's papers caught up with him, when it was learned by the commanding officer in the administration office that he was a landscape architect, Gareth was reassigned to a nearby convalescent hospital converted from a luxury resort hotel, and placed in charge of the extensive gardens.

In a more congenial atmosphere and with work that used his talent and abilities, Gareth had more time to himself. Many of his off-duty hours were spent in the chaplain's library, as well as in the hospital chapel.

Morning and evening he went to the chapel to quiet the turmoil in his heart, to pray earnestly for peace, for Brooke's safety and their being reunited. Day after day he surrendered his life, his dreams, his hopes for the world, for himself, for his future life with Brooke. Sometimes he felt himself enveloped in a powerful sense of peace. Other times he felt dull and unrefreshed. But he continued to meditate and pray.

One weekend, given leave, Gareth took the bus to Santa Barbara to visit his Grandmother Blythe, and in a spontaneous moment of intimacy Gareth confided some of his true feelings, his doubts and uncertainties, even what he suspected might be a lack of faith.

They had been sitting together out on her balcony, the balmy ocean breeze rustling the leaves of the trees that shaded her yard. The scene was so beatific, it was hard to imagine that battles were raging elsewhere in the world.

Suddenly Gareth broke the peaceful silence. "I don't know, Grandmother. Sometimes I wonder if I did the right thing, if any of it really counts. Sometimes I worry I might lose my faith."

"No, dear boy, you're not losing it. You are being tested. Faith doesn't come whole cloth, permanently—not to anyone, if I'm not mistaken. Always there is some struggle. We read Scripture, listen to sermons, study, hear other people's testimonies. I believe it is a lifelong search—a rewarding one nonetheless. And every once in a while we get the encouragement of an 'Aha!'—an enlightening. Then we know we have a glimpse of God's mercy and his love for us." Gareth tucked away that bit of wisdom from his grandmother with the letter from Aunt Kitty. They kept him going when the going got rough.

chapter
14

NIKI SAT ON THE EDGE of her chair, feeling uncomfortable in her new WRENS uniform. Its collar was rubbing the back of her neck bare, because she had pulled her unruly curls up and tucked them into a twist under the brim of her hat.

Everything had happened so quickly, her head was reeling. After all these months of waiting she had received an official letter to appear for indoctrination. Now here she was to receive her assignment. Excitement stirred within her. At last she could get into the action.

"You will be assigned as a teleprinter operator."

Niki tried to contain her disappointment. Assigned to a dull office job!

The interview seemed to be at an end. Still, the officer was viewing Niki critically, her sharp gaze running up and down her as if taking her measurements. Hesitantly Niki got to her feet, wondering if she should salute, although she wasn't sure quite how, or what to do next.

A few hours later she was on a train with other recruits, traveling on her way to WRENS headquarters, which were fifty miles from London. Upon arrival a poker-faced officer herded them from the train station up the hill to an old resort hotel requisitioned as a dormitory for servicewomen.

The next few days passed in a daze for Niki. The teleprinter was a combination of typewriter and telephone and looked ridiculously impossible to learn. At first she felt completely daunted by it, and she spent the first two days looking over other operators' shoulders, totally confused. However, it had a standard keyboard, and since Niki was quick and bright, little by little she soon learned the basics of using it. Within three weeks she was sitting at her own machine and, tentatively at first, able to receive and send messages.

Her roommates were a mixture of types. Elly, a small, slender blond with a pretty face and friendly manner, became Niki's comrade. They hit it off right away, and her friendship made Niki feel a little less adrift.

Those first weeks in the WRENS were filled with getting used to everything—the rigid schedule, the institutional food, the job, and the other women. Niki had little time to herself. She was so tired at night, she fell into her bunk exhausted, and it seemed she had hardly slept when it was time to get up again and report to duty.

Gradually she became accustomed to her new way of life. It was then she faced another new and unexpected challenge.

For the first time in all the months she had been away, Niki was having bouts of homesickness. The summer in France had been too full of new sights, experiences, and adventures for her to feel any twinges. When she returned to England, she had been too excited at the prospect of joining some branch of the service to help fight the war. But now she found her thoughts often turning to Mayfield, especially to Montclair.

In the narrow bunk at night she would imagine how it was in Virginia just now. October in Virginia, maples lighting up the landscape with scarlet leaves against the dark green pines. Sun-splashed days with clouds scudding across the blue expanse of sky. She would think of her own bedroom there, and the memory would bring quick tears. Squeezing her eyes tight, she would bring it back, the dear familiarity of the room, the late-autumn golden sunlight flooding in through the windows, her desk and bookshelves, the faded flowered-chintz chair where she used to curl up on rainy days and read romantic novels. The view from her window of the barn where her horse was stabled. Did Maggie miss her? she wondered. Was Tante exercising her? No use pretending. She missed it all much more than she ever dreamed she would.

In December the weather was miserable, and Niki experienced the most dreadful bout of homesickness yet. She missed everything, and with Christmas approaching, she remembered Christmases at Montclair when she and Luc were both little. Tante would supervise the trimming of the tree Uncle Kip had cut on the land and brought in to be set up in its traditional place in the curve of the staircase. Then she and Luc would hang their crudely made decorations—the red paper Santas, the green sawtooth trees, the bells and reindeer, the popcorn strings, tissue paper bells, miniature sleighs, red felt poinsettias—and spread white cotton around the base of the tree, sprinkled with glittering dust that always came off on the rug.

In her memory, that last Christmas she was at home seemed the loveliest of all. She especially remembered Christmas dinner, when they were all gathered round the dinner table, not realizing that this would be the last Christmas they would all be together. Candlelight softened and blurred the elaborate centerpiece of pine cones, pyracantha, and holly. Tall red candles shed their glow on the table set with holly-patterned Lennox china, used only during the holidays. The candlelight sparkled on graceful crystal goblets and heavy silver service. Niki saw it pictured in her mind like a soft-edged Victorian painting of an old-fashioned family scene—sentimental, nostalgic, and unrealistic.

Two weeks before Christmas a notice appeared on the bulletin board, announcing that a committee was forming to plan a Christmas party. A sign-up sheet was attached. Niki glanced at it briefly as she and Elly came off duty one afternoon. Christmas here in this bleak building with people she hardly knew held little interest for Niki. It made her feel even more isolated. Elly, who had been in the WRENS longer and therefore had more seniority, had received a week's leave to go home for the holidays. Niki wouldn't be eligible for more than a three-day pass. But where would she go, what would she do with that? There wasn't time to get down to Birchfields. Schedules being what they were nowadays, she would probably spend Christmas sitting in a crowded train most of the way, then have to turn right around and come back.

Another afternoon Elly and Niki went to play some Ping-Pong in the rec room, which was now decorated with paper chains and a Christmas tree of sorts. Even though Niki acknowledged this attempt at cheerfulness, to her it only made the room look even more bleak and was a reminder of all that she missed of Christmases past.

As they went to pick up their paddles and get balls out of the game box, Niki noticed that some of the Wrens were entertaining company. Several young men in uniform were grouped around the upright piano, where one girl was playing Christmas carols. "For Pete's sake, do you want to have us all bawlin'?" someone shouted. This was followed by scattered laughter, and then someone went to the phonograph and put on some records. Soon the room was filled with lively dance tunes, providing a musical background to Elly and Niki's game.

Niki was about to return one of Elly's serves when someone caught the ball. She turned and saw a tall young man standing to her left, smiling down at her.

"Good evening, Miss. Would you care to dance?" asked a voice with the faintest suggestion of a Scottish burr. She looked up into a pair of merry blue eyes. There was a mixture of shyness and confidence in his expression that she immediately found appealing. He was in an army uniform, but she didn't recognize his rank or insignia. He was broad-shouldered, with thick, reddish blond hair and an engaging smile.

"Care to dance?" he repeated.

"Go ahead, Niki," Elly said, smiling, from the other end of the Ping-Pong table. Niki put down her paddle and took the hand the young solider had offered, and they started to dance.

"I'm a little out of practice," he apologized as they moved out onto the floor. It took a few false steps to get into the rhythm, but then they managed quite well. By the second number they were dancing smoothly together. The third piece began, and it was the popular ballad "Where or When." As they began to dance to it, he said, "You know, those words fit somehow. Now, don't think I'm crazy, but when I first saw you, I had the strangest feeling that we'd already met somewhere. . . ." At Niki's lifted eyebrow he grinned. "Honest, it's not a line. I *did*. By the way, I'm Fraser Montrose."

Montrose! The name gave her a shock. But then, he was from Scotland and that's where the family originated. It was probably as common a name as Smith or Jones was in the States. Before she had a chance to remark on it, someone came to the door of the rec room and called, "Gilbreaux, you've got a phone call."

"That's me. Excuse me," Niki said and hurried out of the room into the hall, still puzzled by the coincidence of the tall stranger's familiar name. When she picked up the phone and heard the voice on the other end of the line, all other thoughts vanished.

It was *Luc.*

She practically screamed his name. "Luc! Where are you? What are you doing?"

"I just got here a few weeks ago. Been getting what they call acclimation briefing. Like we don't understand English." He laughed. "It's *the* English, the Brits, we don't understand. We don't speak the same language, I'm beginning to think."

It was so wonderful to hear Luc's voice with its familiar Virginia drawl, to know that her beloved foster brother was on English soil. Niki could hardly contain her joy. They talked rapidly for a few more excited minutes. Then Luc said, "Now what you've got to do is wrangle a pass. Plead the fact that we are long-lost sister and brother, a long way from home, who need to spend some time together during the holidays."

"Oh, I don't know if I can, Luc. They're awfully strict—"

"Tell them it's a family emergency," he coached. "Maybe we can get down to Birchfields. I've talked to Aunt Garnet, and she and Bryanne want us to come. Seems Steven may get leave. But if we can't do that, at least we can have a little Christmas celebration ourselves."

Niki promised to try. After getting a number where she could reach him in London, she hung up and went straight to her commanding officer to obtain a pass. In her excited state, she completely forgot about the redheaded Scotsman with the strangely familiar name, awaiting her return in the rec room. All that mattered was getting to London to see Luc.

Fraser waited, his eyes glued to the rec room doorway. But Niki didn't come back. Too bad. He would have liked to get to know her. No time. He was shipping out tomorrow to Cornwall for extensive training. He shrugged. Just one of those things. One of those wartime things.

chapter

15

LUC MET NIKI as she got off the train. At her first sight of him, looking terribly handsome and fit, Niki dissolved into happy tears.

"Hey, hey, none of that!" he ordered in a strict voice. "This is supposed to be a joyous reunion. Besides, you're getting my brand-new uniform all damp." The sound of his familiar laugh soon dried Niki's eyes, and when he tucked her arm through his, she had to almost run to keep up with his long-legged stride.

They went to lunch, then walked together along the streets. London was jammed with other young people, mostly all in uniform. Niki felt proud and happy in hers and to be with such a good-looking companion in his American Air Corps uniform.

Luc had tickets to a music hall performance featuring the popular English songstress Vera Lyn. They listened to her melodious rendition of several sentimental ballads, all of which received resounding applause and even standing ovations from the enthusiastic crowd composed mostly of service men and women. Romantic songs like "I Can't Begin to Tell You," "It Had to Be You," "Always," sent tingles all through Niki. Somehow they all reminded her of Paul and that special time together at Birchfields. She wondered where he was now and if he ever thought of her. She glanced at Luc, wondering if there was any special romantic interest in his life. Up until now he had never had one girlfriend very long. Luc just seemed to be enjoying the show, not looking nostalgic or wistful. However, girls had always been crazy about him, especially Niki's Mayfield friends. Casting another glance at Luc's handsome profile, Niki decided that English girls would no doubt have the same reaction.

After the show, they went to supper at an Italian restaurant, then on to a club, where they danced on a floor the size of a postage stamp. It was after two when Luc took Niki to the hotel where he had somehow managed to get her a room, before he returned to the officers' club where he was billeted.

The next day, Niki took full advantage of the luxury of a long bath with no time limit posted on the door. She didn't even have to scrub the tub afterward, as she did at the dorm. Luc was in the lobby, waiting for her so they could spend the day sightseeing.

The last afternoon, before Luc put her on the train to go back, he suggested that they go to Saint Paul's Cathedral. "Uncle Jeff has always talked about the Holman Hunt painting *The Light of the World* that hangs there. He said it is magnificent, one of the best examples of the Pre-Raphaelite artists' work."

Niki had never known too much about painting. Of course, she knew that Scotty Cameron's half brother, Jeff Montrose, was a well-known artist. But she had never been particularly interested in art. But that afternoon something happened.

In the shadowy interior the painting seemed luminous, as though lit by an ethereal light. The figure of Christ, realistically rendered, stood with one hand holding a lantern, the other hand knocking at a closed door.

Niki, accustomed to portrayals of Christ on Sunday school flannel boards or distant stained-glass windows, whispered, "I don't understand. What is it supposed to mean?"

Luc explained in a quiet voice, "The door is supposed to represent the human heart. If you'll notice, there is no latch. Hunt meant to say that it has to be opened from within."

After Luc moved on, exploring other aisles of the church, Niki remained standing before the painting, profoundly moved by it. It was different from anything she had seen or felt before in her life. It was as if she stood on the other side of that door on which Christ was knocking. All her life, and particularly recently, it seemed to her she had been knocking on closed doors. Trying to find out who she was, where she came from, where she truly belonged. She understood what it felt like to be refused entrance. All at once she was reminded of her own indifference to spiritual things. Of course she had gone to church; Tante had always made sure she and Luc attended regularly. But it hadn't really meant that much to her. She thought of the nuns at the orphanage. They had devoted their whole lives to children and women abandoned by society. She thought of Aunt Kitty, who dedicated herself to making people aware of the horrors of war. Niki realized that most of the time, she had been wrapped up in her own self-centeredness. She hadn't really prayed about finding her true parents. After all, God knew who they were and where. But Niki realized she hadn't diligently sought his help.

She realized she didn't really know how to go about seeking him. But as she stood there, something stirred within her. The simple words sprang into her mind spontaneously: *Show me how to open that door. I want you to come in.*

What seemed to come in was some kind of inner voice: *"When you know who you are, I will show you what to do."* Niki stiffened, glanced around. Had someone spoken? What followed was a kind of peace, an assurance that her spontaneous prayer had been heard and an answer had come.

That was it. A few minutes later Luc joined her, saying they had better scout up a taxi to get to the station so she didn't miss her train. Everything snapped back to the present. The experience was over, yet something lingered in Niki that she was determined not to lose.

Mad confusion reigned at the huge train station. Throngs of travelers, scores of uniformed men of all services and ranks, were shoulder-to-shoulder with civilians, among them women and children seeing their loved ones off. Luc, holding Niki tightly by the arm, shoved their way through to where she would have to board. Shortness of time turned their parting to a hasty good-bye.

On the station platform, Luc gave her a bear hug and steered her into one of the already crowded compartments crammed with service men and women. "Thanks, Luc, for a wonderful time!" Niki shouted over the noise. Suddenly her throat felt choked. When would they see each other again? The reality of the war suddenly struck her. But Luc's voice was firm, optimistic, as he yelled back, "Maybe we'll see each other at Birchfields next. In the meantime, take care. And Happy New Year!" *That's right*, Niki thought, *it is a new year. Nineteen forty-three. What would it bring? Peace?*

Bumping back to WRENS headquarters on the crowded, hot, smoky, stuffy train, the magic time in London with Luc seemed like a dream.

For the most part they had been cheerful. They hadn't talked of anything serious; they had laughed a lot. Now Niki wondered if maybe they should have talked of more important things—how they felt about each other, about home, about Tante and Uncle Kip, about poor, shackled France and what was happening to England.

By the time she reached her destination, it was after midnight. There had been many stops, scheduled and unscheduled, along the way. Once the train had been stopped, the passengers evacuated, because of an air-raid alarm. The attack hadn't come, but they'd had to wait, huddled in a small airless shelter until the all clear was sounded. Back on the train, they had racketed down the tracks. To her amazement Niki fell asleep and awoke with a jerk when the train came to a screeching stop.

Plodding upstairs to her quarters, she found her roommates asleep. As she stumbled her way along in the dark, her arrival evoked sleepy grumbles. Trying not to trip over the rug, Niki made her way through the pile of dumped belongings that the last one in had dropped in the middle of the room, before falling exhausted into her own bunk.

1943

chapter

16

NIKI FOUND THAT although she was getting better at her job as a teleprinter operator, she felt restless, longed for more interesting work.

When she was off duty, she haunted bookstores, both new and secondhand, searching for French-language books, grammar and phrase books mostly, but then for works of fiction. More and more she was thinking in French. That, she knew, was a good sign. It meant she was becoming more familiar with it.

Weeks went by, the situation in Europe worsened, and Niki began to chafe under the routine she now considered dull and prosaic, given the possibility of what she might be allowed to do.

Then one weekend, feeling particularly restless and frustrated, she asked for a weekend pass and to her surprise got it. She decided to go down to Birchfields. With its rolling hills, trees, and quiet lake where swans floated gracefully, it seemed the only place left with the serene beauty of prewar England.

Garnet was always happy to see her, and Bryanne welcomed an extra pair of hands for the evening of hostessing the men who flocked over to enjoy Garnet's openhearted hospitality. Niki availed herself of the chance of a leisurely bath, rather guiltily dumping quantities of scented bath salts into the deliciously warm water. Months of the regulation five-minute showers had made her appreciative of such a rare luxury.

Relaxed and refreshed, Niki came downstairs Friday evening, hearing the sound of dance music, and saw couples already circling the polished floors of the drawing room and hallway, where rugs had been rolled up for dancing. Men in every conceivable kind of uniform stood watching the dancers, waiting to cut in, for there were always more of them than available female partners.

It was then that Niki saw him. He was standing in the archway, talking to a fellow officer. There was something vaguely familiar about him. Even as she was trying to recall just why, he turned and looked at her. A smile of recognition broke across his face, and he half raised his hand in greeting. In another minute he was striding toward her. As he got closer, she saw he was above medium height, well-built, wearing a British uniform whose insignia she did not recognize. He wasn't handsome—his nose was too prominent in his lean, high-cheekboned face, the chin too square—but his smile lit up his very blue eyes, which were regarding her with interest and humor.

When he reached her, he said, "I had a feeling we'd meet again"—using the words of the popular song, he sang the rest—"'don't know where, don't know when . . .'" He grinned. "Did *you?*"

His voice, with its slight Scottish burr, clicked in her memory. Where or when had they met?

Before it came to her, he spoke again. "WRENS headquarters in December. I'm Fraser Montrose, and you are—Gilbert, isn't it?"

"Gilbreaux." Niki automatically gave it the softer French pronunciation.

"We danced and then you had a phone call." His smile turned into a teasing grin. "And you never came back."

"I'm sorry. That was very rude of me. I should have explained."

"Not necessary. Luckily, we have another chance to get acquainted. Could we find some place to sit down and talk?"

Just then, over Fraser's shoulder Niki saw Bryanne beckoning her, signaling she needed her at the refreshment table.

"Excuse me, I'm supposed to be helping here tonight."

"I didn't realize. I thought you were here on R and R." He looked puzzled. "Are you a local girl?"

"Not exactly—" Niki hesitated.

Fraser gave her a curious look.

"Listen, I'll go do my chore, and then I'll bring us some punch and we can talk, OK?"

"Promise not to disappear again?"

"I promise," Niki said, laughing, and hurried away.

Twenty minutes later, after she had refilled the punch bowl and got dozens more cookies from the kitchen, arranged them on a tray, and placed them on the long refreshment table, she looked around for Fraser. He was sitting in one of the alcoved window seats in the drawing room. Carrying two cups of punch, she went to join him. When she handed him one, Fraser said, "You know, you're a bit of a mystery, and I love mystery novels, crossword puzzles, so I've ferreted a little out about you. But you'll have to fill in the blanks."

Niki wasn't ready to pour out her whole life story to a stranger, even an attractive one. So she countered, "Well, you're almost as much a mystery to me. Tell me about *you*."

"Not much to tell. I'm twenty-four, was at the University of Edinburgh, not quite sure what I planned to do, when the war came about. So I joined up and now I'm in special training. Can't be specific about what kind. But since you're in the service, you can understand that. That's about it. Nothing mysterious about me."

"Of course, I knew you were a Scot by your accent . . ."

"And you have an accent yourself," Fraser said. "I can't figure out whether it's American or—Canadian, maybe?"

Niki rolled her eyes. "Hardly!"

"It's not Australian. I bunk with some Aussies, and I can tell it's not that."

"Have you heard of Virginia?"

"Of course. I have relatives there. In fact, my father was an American from Virginia." He frowned. "From a little town you've probably never heard of, Mayfield."

"Heard of it? I live there!"

"Gilbreaux? That doesn't sound American to me," Fraser said slowly.

"It isn't. It's French. My real parents were French. But my adopted parents are American, and their name is Montrose."

There was a moment of stunned silence. They simply stared at each other. Then they both started talking at once. In a jumble of words, interrupting each other with questions, they sorted out the puzzle. Fraser was Jonathan Montrose's son by his second marriage, to Phoebe McPherson.

"So we're related!" Fraser said. Then he sounded disappointed. "I don't know whether to be glad or sorry."

Niki had to laugh. "Well, not really. However, Virginians go to unbelievable lengths to claim kinship. I'm not actually a Montrose, so we're not even what they call 'kissin' cousins.'"

Fraser drew his face into a comical one. "Now, I *know* I'm disappointed about *that*."

Niki laughed. "You're really funny. I thought all Scotsmen were dour."

"That's as much a misconception as the idea that all Southern women live on plantations and are pampered belles."

"I guess we both have a lot to learn about each other."

"That will be a great deal of fun." Fraser smiled. "By the way, I meant to introduce myself to Mrs. Devlin when I first came tonight. Then I saw you and got sidetracked. My mum wrote to her that if I were stationed anywhere near Birchfields, I would come by, pay my respects. Would you like to take me to her?"

"She may have already gone upstairs. She usually only stays for about the first half hour of the evening. She's very old, you know," Niki said, glancing around the crowded room for a glimpse of Garnet. "But of course you'll come again, and she will insist you make Birchfields your home away from home. Now *she* is a true Southern lady and was, I'm told, a true belle in her day."

"Then, another time," Fraser said. He tipped his head to one side, saying, "Listen . . ." The song "Where or When" was playing. "I don't think we ever finished our dance. Shall we?"

They moved onto the dance floor and danced surprisingly well together. When the music ended, Niki said, "I'm sorry, I have to go. As one of the hostesses, I'm supposed to circulate, make sure every guy who wants to gets a chance to dance."

Fraser had no choice. He watched her walk away, thinking what a pretty and delightful young woman she was. What a coincidence the two meetings with her had been.

Maybe it was even more of a coincidence than either realized.

Saturday evening Fraser was at Birchfields again, eager to get to know Niki better. She was undoubtedly the most intriguing young woman he had ever met. He walked through the French doors into the drawing room, which had now been turned into a sort of cabaret, with small tables all around the edge of a dance space that had been cleared, stripped of carpeting, and waxed. He stood on the threshold for a minute or two, his glance searching the room.

He saw her before she saw him. He started across the room, but before he reached her, an American had whirled her out onto the floor.

Impatiently Fraser waited until the piece was over, then in a few quick strides reached Niki's side.

"I believe the next one is mine," he said confidently to the airman. "Sorry, buddy."

"Hello," Niki said, smiling up at him.

At least she looked happy to see him.

If she also looked a little dazed, it was because as Niki had seen Fraser approach, something startling had happened. As distinctly as if she had heard them spoken, these words came into Niki's mind: *Someday he will tell me he loves me.* Nothing like that had ever happened to her before, and as Fraser tapped the other soldier's arm and smiled at her, it seemed even more strange.

This is crazy, she thought. *My imagination is working over-time.* This rangy Scot with the reddish blond hair wasn't even her type. Too American-looking, actually. Her romantic fantasies ran more to the dark-eyed, Gallic kind, like Paul Duval.

The strains of "The Last Time I Saw Paris" began, and Fraser took Niki into his arms.

As the evening wore on and they enjoyed dance after dance together, Niki found herself strongly attracted to Fraser. Those strange predictive words floated back to her: *Someday he will tell me he loves me.*

But not yet. Not for a long while. . . .

At last the band began playing its last number, and Fraser asked, "Will you still be here on Sunday? Could we do something together?"

Sunday morning when Niki came out of church with Aunt Garnet and Bryanne, Fraser was waiting for her. Flustered, she introduced them. Both Garnet and Bryanne were taken aback. "My stars, what a surprise!" exclaimed the old lady.

Bryanne expressed her surprise as well. "The last time I saw you, you were just a gangly kid!"

"You should have let me know you were stationed so close," Garnet said.

"Actually, mum didn't know. Mail moves slowly in wartime and I just got my orders." Fraser had the grace to look embarrassed. "I'm afraid I'm not much good at letter writing."

Garnet wagged a playful finger at him. "You should be ashamed. Don't you know how anxious she must be about you?" Her smile softened her words. "I think I'll write her myself and tell her how delighted I am to have met you."

After an exchange of recent happenings, information, Garnet insisted that Fraser come back to Birchfields with them for "a family reunion of sorts."

Back at the house, they sat down to a luncheon of poached salmon, new potatoes, and lemon pudding. Garnet looked at Fraser affectionately as she told him how dear his father, Jonathan, had been to her.

"After my sister-in-law, Rose, died, I took care of Jonathan until he was nearly six years old and went to live with his Meredith relatives in Massachusetts." Garnet wiped her eyes. "That was one of the saddest days of my life, to part with the little boy that I'd come to think of as mine."

"Thank you, Mrs. Devlin. That's most kind."

"Mrs. Devlin, nonsense! Aunt Garnet," she corrected him. "And you are to make yourself completely at home here, you understand?"

Fraser looked at Niki on the other side of the table and grinned. She met his gaze, then lowered her eyes demurely. She remembered her hesitation in telling him who she was, explaining their strange relationship. Now the cat was out of the bag, so to speak. Perhaps now Fraser would be here at Birchfields with or without her encouragement. Not that she minded. . . . She lifted her eyes and glanced over at him. He was still looking at her. She felt her cheeks get warm.

Bryanne, her own whirlwind romance still so sweetly fresh in her mind, spotted a potential one almost at once. She lent them Steven's Bentley and her petrol ration card and told them to go off for the day.

It was one of those days that would become a cherished memory, Niki thought even as they drove away from Birchfields. The sky was an unclouded blue, and everything seemed incredibly beautiful. The winding country lanes, the rolling hills where black-faced sheep grazed contentedly. It seemed so peaceful. How was it possible that only a short distance from where the little car took the curves, men were killing each other? Niki thrust that thought fiercely back. Not today. Today she would enjoy the moment.

Fraser glanced over at her and smiled. He had taken off his cap, and his thick hair blew wildly. She smiled back. In fact, she found she couldn't do anything but smile.

After a while they came to a village. Fraser slowed down and asked her if she wanted to stop for tea. He swerved and parked, and across the street they saw a sign: "Buttercup Tea Shop." Niki smothered a giggle. It was one of those places she made fun of as being "so tea-cozy British." She had always described them with her wickedly derisive humor as "those places where elderly women gather to gossip and discuss the latest diet while ordering fluffy desserts." Today, however, its quaint atmosphere seemed just right, delightful in fact. All her humorous comments faded into oblivion as they came inside the charming interior and Fraser found a table for them in a corner.

"Alone at last." He grinned. "Now I intend to find out all about you."

Niki looked at him, all wide-eyed innocence. "But I've told you everything there is to know."

"Not by a long shot. Why do you use the name Gilbreaux?" he asked. "Why not Montrose? Didn't your adopted mother's husband adopt you, too?"

"It's rather a long story . . . ," she hedged.

"We've got all afternoon and I'd really like to hear. Don't you know, Niki, that everything about you interests me?"

The question was left hanging between them, because the waitress came to take their order. When she left, Fraser leaned forward again. "So now, carry on. You are hiding behind the name Gilbreaux because you're some kind of Mata Hari, a spy, perhaps?"

"Nothing that glamorous or exciting, I'm afraid." She drew a long breath. "Well, if you really want to know. I had always used Tante's name before I went to France the summer of 1939. My intention was to go to the orphanage where I was brought as a baby and find out about my real parents."

"And did you?"

Niki shook her head and again stopped as their waitress brought them a pot of tea, two cups and saucers, then went away again. Niki poured and as she did, she wondered how she could explain all this to Fraser. Or why she now agreed that it was important that he know more about her.

"What happened then? I mean, in France?" Fraser asked.

"I went to the orphanage—well, it's no longer an orphanage, but I thought they would have records or something about who brought me there, so I might be able to trace my real parents."

"And?" Fraser prompted.

"It wasn't much help." Niki shook her head. "The nun in charge told me that after the war there was a lot of confusion. Nobody seemed to know or care much about records and birth certificates. The children just needed shelter, food—"

"Did they tell you anything?"

"She showed me a list of possible last names, one of which was Gilbreaux. But she did not know whether the woman who brought me there was my real mother or a relative or perhaps some kind person who found me abandoned somewhere. That seems to have happened often in those dreadful times. Even if the parents loved their child, they may have had no way to support their little one. Who knows? So you see, I don't know who I am or where I come from."

"I'm sorry."

"Anyway, I decided to use the name Gilbreaux. I thought it would be easier to get into one of the services. That was, of course, before Pearl Harbor and the Americans coming in."

The waitress came back with their food, and they both realized they were hungry. While they ate toasted cheese sandwiches and tomatoes, they turned to lighter subjects. The waitress suggested fresh apple tart for dessert, and Fraser ordered another pot of tea.

When it came, he filled their cups, then said to Niki, "You know, asking you about yourself was not just idle curiosity. I'm really interested. And from what you've told me, I'd say you were one of the lucky ones, to have had someone like Cara to love and want you, give you an obviously wonderful home. Many of the orphans there probably spent most of their childhood in institutions—"

"You're saying I should be grateful instead of looking for my real parents, changing my name." Niki's dark eyes flashed. "But you can't understand about this emptiness, this not knowing, all the missing pieces. You can't know how that feels. So telling me how I should feel is pointless."

"Forgive me." Contrite, Fraser reached across the table for Niki's hand. "I only meant that at least you grew up in a home with two parents who loved you, cared for you—"

"I didn't mean to sound ungrateful. Tante and Kip—the Montroses—are wonderful. So is my foster brother, Luc. He's half French, too, so we understand each other." She broke off. "I've talked enough about myself."

There was so much more Fraser longed to know about her, but sensing her mood, he decided it would have to wait for another time. It was enough for now. She was the most interesting girl he had ever met. He felt in his heart of hearts that he and Niki Gilbreaux had a lot more to find out about one another, things that had nothing to do with the Montrose family. They were linked in a very different way. But now it was wartime. Everything that had to do with the future had to be postponed. Still, he knew that he and Niki, somewhere down the line, had discoveries to make together.

Fraser's train was already in the station when they arrived, so there wasn't much time left together. As Niki stood with him on the platform, Fraser asked, "I want to see you again. Like the song says, where or when?"

"Well, I have to get back to my job."

"If I come up to London?"

"Sure. If I don't have duty."

"I'll call," he said. The train whistle gave a warning shriek, but Fraser remained standing, looking down at Niki.

"You'd better hurry," she said.

Fraser took a few steps away from her, then turned back, and before she could move, he put his hands on her upper arms and drew her close, waited a single second, then leaned down and kissed her. It seemed so natural a thing to do that Niki didn't even blink but returned his kiss.

"I'll call!" he said as he started down the platform to the nearest train car. He waved again before swinging aboard.

"Yes, do that!" Niki called back and stood there waving until the train had disappeared down the track. Then she walked slowly back to where she had left the Bentley. It was getting dark as she drove up the road back to Birchfields. The lovely old mansion was silhouetted against the purplish sky. Everything looked the same, but for Niki everything had changed. She felt different. Something strange and wonderful had happened. She wasn't sure just what . . . yet.

chapter
17

NIKI HAD TO CATCH an early train the morning after Fraser left, and as she traveled back to WRENS headquarters, she tried to make some sense out of the last few days. The unbelievable connection of their lives, the almost instant camaraderie they had, the ease with which she had been able to talk to him, even to tell him so much about herself, amazed her. Could you get to know someone well enough that quickly to imagine yourself in love? People were always talking about love at first sight. Did that really happen? Or was it just wartime? They said it happened because everyone was desperate to grab whatever happiness they could while they could. But Niki hadn't felt that way. She just wanted the war to be over, for France to be free again, so she could go back, pick up her search to find her real parents.

Fraser had made her realize how lucky she was to have been brought up in such a loving family. She had never actually compared her good fortune with the fate of the other babies who had been brought to the orphanage at the same time she had. What had become of them? Where were they now?

Niki shivered and shifted her cramped position in the crowded compartment of the train. She looked around her at the other men and women in uniform. What would happen to them, to us all? she wondered. And to her and Fraser, who out of the strangest of coincidences in this crazy, mixed-up world had found each other?

Elly was lying on her bunk reading when Niki came into their quarters. She looked up from her book and stared at Niki curiously. "What's happened to you?"

"What do you mean? I just spent nearly four uncomfortable hours on a train and then a bus, that's what happened to me," Niki replied wearily, dropping her duffel bag and sinking down on the bunk opposite.

"No, not that. . . . There's something different about you." Elly looked puzzled.

Niki almost said, "I'm in love." But she didn't have a chance, because Elly yawned and said, "You're to report to Officer Brimley, first thing."

"Now?"

"Now." Elly returned to her book.

Niki grabbed a quick cup of strong tea, laced heavily with sugar to give her some much needed energy, before reporting to her superior.

As she entered the office, Officer Brimley glanced up briefly from whatever she was writing. Frowning, she acknowledged Niki's salute, then continued filling out what looked to Niki like a long requisition sheet. Finally she raised her head and gave Niki a measuring look.

"We have received a communiqué stating you may qualify for a special assignment," Officer Brimley said briskly. "You are granted a two-day pass to go to London for an interview with Colonel Thornton. You are to leave as soon as you can arrange transportation."

Niki blinked. "That's all, ma'am?"

"That's all." Officer Brimley's lips closed in a firm line, and she handed Niki a slip of paper.

Niki had been in the service long enough to know that one was given only necessary information, no more. "Yours is just to do or die." Still, she was full of curiosity. What did this mean? What kind of special assignment?

She still felt stiff, sandy-eyed, from her trip. Now she was supposed to turn around and go back to London.

Niki arrived in London an hour earlier than her appointment and had time for a quick cup of tea and a few biscuits at the station tearoom before reporting to the address she was given. It was a plain office building with no indication of what it housed. She gave her name at the receptionist's desk in the front hall and was taken upstairs and into an office. Behind a large desk were two army officers, who rose to their feet at her entrance. Niki was so astonished that she forgot to salute as she had been taught in basic training.

What followed was even more strange. One of the officers, a man with rugged features, an outdoorsy complexion, and a gray mustache, introduced himself. "I'm Colonel Thornton. This is Captain Strawn." He indicated the officer standing to his right. "We appreciate your coming. You are probably asking yourself just why you have been singled out." He paused. "We understand you speak and comprehend French fluently. We are looking for bilinguals, because of the present situation in France."

An hour later Niki left the office, went down the stairs and back into the hallway. Just as she was about to push through the outside doors, something caused her to halt, look back over her shoulder. It was then that something stopped her cold. Coming out one of the doors behind her was a man who seemed familiar. Niki didn't recognize the blue gray uniform he was wearing; however, he was deep in conversation with a British officer. As they walked together down the hall toward her, she saw that the officer was Captain Strawn, who had excused himself and left during her interview.

Niki stood there, her hand on the door handle, ready to walk outside. The closer they approached, the surer she became. His name formed itself on her lips and she was about to call it out, when he lifted his head and their gaze met. It lasted only a split second, for he whirled around abruptly and started walking back down the hall. The officer with him looked startled, then glanced over at Niki and followed the other man more slowly until he caught up with him at the end of the corridor. They both disappeared into the door of an office.

Niki was bewildered. Her brain signaled that she had not been mistaken. The man with Captain Strawn was Paul Duval. She was sure it was he. What was he doing in London? Why had he not contacted her? But then, she hadn't heard a word from him since that last night at Birchfields, the night they had danced on the terrace and he had kissed her. . . . The romantic aura of that evening seemed in stark contrast to the reality of this austere building, London at war. Had he seen her? If so, why had he turned around and gone in the other direction as if . . . as if what? Was he avoiding her? Avoiding being seen and recognized? But why? She gave her head a little shake as if to clear it. She went out and walked a few blocks. It *was* Paul. She *knew* it was Paul.

Niki stopped short. She was walking in the wrong direction. She should be going toward Victoria station to catch her train. She reversed herself, still lost in thought. What was Paul doing in that building? She had taken an oath of silence about the purpose of her interview, because the attempt to enlist bilingual people to set up radio contacts in occupied France was top secret. Did Paul have something to do with that? Was Paul part of the French Resistance, here in London on some secret mission?

Suddenly Niki felt a hundred years old. This was not the exciting adventure she had at first imagined. Stories were surfacing every day of Nazi occupation, of atrocities, of torture and betrayals. With certainty she knew Paul was involved in this underground movement against the oppressors.

She thought of the studied politeness of her interview. After questioning her at some length, Colonel Thornton had said, "Well, we are grateful for your coming, for your candor in replying to all our inquiries into your personal life. You are, however, quite young, and this is a great responsibility, requiring much thought and intensive training of a very different sort from what you've undergone in the WRENS. I have given you a cursory overview of what would be demanded of someone in this unit. I advise you to think it over very carefully. We will certainly keep your name on file."

He had been courteous but dismissive, and Niki left, subdued and uncertain. Had she bitten off more than she could chew? Would she be up to it if—and that was a big if—they called her back, accepted her for this secret mission? Then Niki remembered what had happened to her at Saint Paul's Cathedral, her new commitment to seek God's guidance, her new conviction that he would give it if she asked.

chapter

18

THREE WOMEN OBSERVED Luc Montrose's arrival as his small English sports car swerved into the graveled circle in front of Birchfields. One was his Great Aunt Garnet, standing at the diamond-paned windows of the library. The other two, Alair Blanding and Cilla Ridgeway, looked from an upstairs bedroom window, partially hidden by the chintz curtains. They leaned on the sill, watching him as he parked the red Austin-mini, then unfolded his long, lean body out of the car. He stood for a minute, running his hand through his dark, wind-tousled hair, before reaching back and retrieving his cap from the seat. He put it on, adjusted the tunic of his U.S. Air Force officer's uniform, and in a few quick strides took the terraced steps of the sprawling Tudor mansion.

The cousins exchanged an approving glance. One girl let out a long, low whistle, rolling her eyes dramatically. The other affected a swoon, sighing. Then they both laughed. They had been curious to meet this young man they had heard so much about from Niki. His photograph was among those in Aunt Garnet's "rogues gallery," as she called the silver-framed family pictures displayed on the piano in her upstairs sitting room. Most of them lived in Virginia, where the girls' step-grandmother Druscilla also lived.

From his adopted sister they had heard that Luc was handsome and charming. Was he also as reckless and headstrong as his father, Kip, the fabled WWI ace?

Alair and Cilla had grown up in England, but because of the American connection, they were always curious about that branch of the family. Since Aunt Garnet had begun having her open weekends for servicemen at the nearby army base, they came to help with the hostessing. As Cilla quipped, "Tough duty, but someone's got to do it!" They enjoyed the flattering attention showered on them by the British servicemen, but since the United States had come into the war, a smattering of Americans training in the area also came to the dances and buffets. Alair had graduated from the Swiss finishing school they had both attended and was teaching at the improvised kindergarten started for some of the London refugee children now posted in various homes in the county. Due to the war, Cilla had not been able to return to Switzerland and was now completing her education at an English girls' school in Kent. Cilla was champing at the bit to enlist in any of the women's service organizations. Volunteering to be hostesses for the weekend events was a "war work" both girls enjoyed tremendously. It required little else than to be gracious and dance well, skills they both had in abundance.

"Shall we go down now or wait until Aunt Garnet calls us?" Alair asked, going over to the dressing table and fluffing her golden hair.

Cilla pulled a comical face. "I don't know. Perhaps we'd better go on our own, appear casual."

Alair checked her wristwatch. "It's almost teatime. It would seem perfectly natural for us to go down now, don't you think?" She couldn't understand her own timidity about meeting this American cousin. Well, not really a cousin. He was actually their step-grandmother Druscilla's cousin or half cousin or something like that!

A half hour later, sitting across the room from Luc, Alair had to admit he was every bit as handsome and charming as Niki had told them. What he was really like under his assured personality and keen sense of humor, she intended to find out. When introduced, he had greeted them both with the kind of ease attributed to well-bred Southerners. His was the more casual type of good manners compared with that of the young Englishmen she knew. And she found it very attractive.

After about fifteen minutes of general conversation, Aunt Garnet excused herself, explaining, "We're shorthanded these days as to the household staff, Luc. The younger people have all gone into various branches of the service. My cook, Mrs. Beasley, takes an afternoon nap and sometimes sleeps through teatime. So I'd better go see if things are ready." She got up from her chair. "Poor soul, she's getting on in years so. . . ."

At this remark Alair and Cilla exchanged a glance. Aunt Garnet, over one hundred years old, never considered herself as "getting on in years." Truly she was a marvel.

Leaving the young people chatting as if they'd known each other forever and had not grown up on opposite sides of the Atlantic, Garnet went out to the kitchen. Over the years she had acquired the English custom of late afternoon tea and now looked forward to it. It was usually just a light snack when she was here alone, but now with Luc and the girls here with their youthful appetites, she wanted to make sure there were plenty of tiny sandwiches, freshly made currant scones, to serve. With so many shortages due to wartime rationing, they were lucky to be in the country, where eggs and butter from nearby farms were readily available. Although doing without such things was not all that much of a sacrifice. Surely, she'd learned to do without a great many more important things during the War between the States. What an awful time that had been at Montclair, when she, Dove, and their children had been left to manage while their husbands were off fighting. But why dwell on that? Garnet scolded herself. She pushed those unpleasant memories to the back of her mind, something that over the years she had learned to do quite skillfully. "Live in the moment" had become her byword. In life there was too much pain, sorrow, loss, that came to you without anticipating it.

Garnet found that Mrs. Beasley was up and, though sleepy-eyed, busily arranging the tea tray. Satisfied, she returned to the library. Of all the rooms in the house, this had been the favorite of Jeremy, her late husband. It had floor-to-ceiling oak bookshelves filled with leather-bound classics, and was furnished with deep, comfortable chairs. Over the mantel hung the painting Jeremy had loved most, a portrait of Garnet and their daughter, painted when Faith was fourteen by a well-known society portrait artist.

Charles, the butler, pushed the tea trolley into its place by Garnet's chair, and she poured the steaming, fragrant liquid into Wedgwood cups. Observing that Luc and Alair were in an animated conversation, she signaled Cilla to pass the plates of thin cucumber, watercress, and creamed-salmon sandwiches around to the others.

Luc helped himself generously to the plate Cilla offered him, while saying to Garnet, "This is a wonderful house, Aunt Garnet. I don't think I noticed it when I was here before. I've been thinking about possibly going into architecture as a profession. That is, I was, before the war."

"Yes, it is lovely. And quite old, but well built. It was constructed in the 1850s, we were told. Craftsmanship was a matter of pride then. It's much too big for a woman living alone, but when we first came here, it was different, of course. We used to do a great deal of entertaining. . . ." Garnet's voice held a trace of melancholy as in her mind's eye she saw the picture of long-ago summer afternoons, the women in their embroidered, lace-trimmed white dresses, veiled hats, the men in blue blazers, stiff collars, white flannels—playing croquet and gathering for tea served underneath the trees.

She glanced over at Luc. She could see in him traces of both his father, Kip, and grandfather, Jonathan, Garnet's beloved "foster son." Underneath the cheerful chatter, Garnet felt a wave of depression and fear. There were so many reminders in this scene. Luc looked so young and confident in his uniform, but behind him rose the specter of other young men in uniform. Confederate gray and Union blue, the khaki of 1914. . . . Garnet suppressed a shudder. It wouldn't do to let the young people see under her facade. She had seen too much of war in her lifetime, what it did to young men, to women who loved them, to families. The first terrible war with Germany still was a scar in her memory. In 1917 she had turned Birchfields into a recuperative center, a place where men could come and be healed—physically and emotionally. It was something she had never thought to do again. Not that she was repeating that effort. Only on the weekends this time, and without the help of Bryanne and others, she would not have been able to do that. But life must go on. One must be cheerful and do what one could.

How long had it taken her to learn that? To accept life, to bow to fate, to become resigned to her losses, her pains, problems, challenges—and also her great happiness. She had known love and had been loved. What more could one ask? She smiled ruefully, thinking, *I sound like Grace Comfort. Maybe I should write a column.* She glanced over at Cilla and a smile lifted her mouth. The fact that Grace Comfort was really Cilla's father, Victor, was the well-guarded family secret.

Then Garnet glanced at Alair, who was listening with rapt

attention to some humorous story Luc was telling. There was an expression on her pretty face that brought a slight stab of recognition to Garnet. She looked dazzled. This was not exactly surprising. Luc was certainly any girl's romantic idol, and the uniform added to the glamour, which often led many to mistake infatuation for love. In wartime so many dangers darkened these quick love affairs. But young people nowadays were more knowledgeable, more sophisticated than in other times, and Alair was a sensible girl, not one to easily let her heart rule her head—at least Garnet hoped not. She felt a responsibility to the girls' mothers, since she had enlisted their daughters to help her hostess these weekend parties.

The best thing was to keep them all busy and moving in a crowd, no pairing off, so they don't get romantic ideas. Garnet turned to Luc and asked, "Did I tell you that Fraser Montrose, from Scotland, is stationed nearby? He came for a visit recently. I practically raised his father, Jonathan, you know. You've met Fraser, haven't you?"

Luc smiled. "You mean my *Uncle* Fraser?"

"Uncle?" echoed Alair, looking puzzled.

"Another of the Montrose family's complicated relationships," Luc explained. "My father and Fraser are half brothers. Jonathan is their father. His first wife—Dad's mother—died, and Grandfather married Phoebe McPherson later and had a second family, Fraser and Fiona."

"Oh, you Virginians! It's so mixed up! I can't keep all these relationships straight." Cilla rolled her eyes as if in exasperation.

"You don't have to," Luc said, grinning. "I was a bit wary when I came over in 1939 and went to Scotland—to get acquainted, you see—but I felt right at home." He smiled at Cilla. "Wait and see. You'll like Fraser."

"Niki will be down this weekend," Garnet said, "and if Fraser comes, it will be a real family reunion. I have an idea."

"What is your idea, Aunt Garnet?" asked Cilla, the practical one.

"Why don't you have a picnic? Make a day of it?" Garnet suggested. She herself had always loved picnics, as a young girl and even after. She loved the informality, the gaiety, that seemed to be a special ingredient of such times.

"Do we have enough petrol?" Luc asked. "I only requisitioned enough to get here and back to the base."

"You can take my station wagon, and no need to go far. There are some lovely spots within a short distance. I'll have Mrs. Beasley pack you a basket."

Niki did not arrive. She called Garnet, and although it was hard to hear with the crackling on the line, Garnet got the message that something had come up and Niki could not come. When Garnet told her Luc was at Birchfields, she sounded very disappointed. But there was no help for it. Wartime, as everyone accepted, made the best plans go awry.

"Well, I hope you'll have better luck next time, honey," Garnet said consolingly.

"So do I," Niki said. Garnet could hear the sadness in her voice. To have missed a weekend at Birchfields was bad enough; to miss seeing Luc was worse.

Neither did Fraser show up. But the other three "cousins" enjoyed themselves anyway.

Since it was Friday and the beginning of the weekend open house at Birchfields, some of the regulars from the airfield came over that evening. Invitations to the picnic were extended to them, as well as to some of Alair's and Cilla's special girlfriends.

The following morning when Luc came downstairs, breakfast was set out in the English manner, and both girls were already at the table. Through the glass French doors a glimpse of the magnificent sweep of green lawns and gardens could be seen. It was such a peaceful scene that it was possible to imagine that there was no such thing as war.

Luc helped himself to the wide selection of dishes, remembering what Aunt Garnet had told him: in the country, the deprivations of wartime were not so obvious. Birchfields raised its own pigs and chickens, so there were grilled sausages, eggs, and jam made from berry bushes in the kitchen garden.

"You've certainly got a day for a picnic," Garnet remarked, stopping in the doorway on her way out to the kitchen to check on the baskets being packed for them. In the pantry, she looked through the cabinets and saw the neatly arranged rows of canned ham, chutneys, jars of marmalade, mustard, luscious preserves. She was glad she'd gone to Fortnum and Mason before she left London last time, and had stocked up on some goodies. When she bought the delicacies, she had not thought about a picnic, but now it seemed the perfect use for them.

She put out her hand for a bright tartan container of Dundee cakes, thinking to include it in the basket. Then she thought better of it. She enjoyed them as her bedtime snack, and since one never knew when they might be scarce, she decided to keep them for herself. Old age has to have some compensations, she thought, chuckling a little at her own joke and her own selfishness. Young people had youth and the possibility of love, which was more than she had and far more enjoyable than cream crackers.

Several of the young men from last night arrived in an overcrowded jeep just as Luc and the girls finished breakfast.

By ten o'clock she had seen them off. The favored airmen piled into the army jeep, and their "dates" crowded into an old jalopy, a relic resurrected by necessity from a wrecking lot. Luc apologized that his Austin-mini had room for only a single passenger. Somehow Alair found herself seated in it. Cilla, at the wheel of Garnet's station wagon—which was loaded with the picnic baskets, blankets, pillows, and a box containing a bad-minton set—took the overflow from the jeep, and the caravan started off amid much laughing and shouting.

The place Garnet had suggested was a lovely tree-shaded glade with a sloping path to a quiet lake. Actually, it was at the end of Birchfields' vast property.

Everyone spilled out of their cramped transportation and scattered to explore the beautiful site. Some of them set up the net for the badminton game, handed out rackets, and chose teams.

The game was fiercely played, hotly competitive, the girls vying to win as the fellows wielded their rackets and sent the shuttlecock soaring over the net with strong strokes.

A great deal of laughter, teasing, challenges, ensued as they argued about points. It was all in good fun and, declaring it a draw, they finally all sought the cool shade under the huge trees. They opened the picnic hampers and started bringing out the food. Lemonade and chilled cider were poured, and everyone ate hungrily of the sandwiches and ham, the fruit and cakes.

The earlier high spirits seemed to gradually dissolve into quiet conversations. Some of the players stretched out on the grass, worn out from the strenuous exercise, lulled by the humming warmth of the afternoon, feeling the unusual relaxation of this peaceful spot. Some even closed their eyes and drifted off.

"All my life I've heard it quoted, 'Oh, to be in England, now that April's here.' Now I know what they mean," Luc said to Alair.

"Yes, it is lovely. Oddly enough, it seems especially so this April," she remarked. "It's so peaceful that it's hard to imagine—"

Luc looked at her with a surprised expression. "You must be reading my mind. That was almost exactly what I was think-ing. That I'm here in England, at this spot, at this particular time in history. Half the world is at war and there are a lot of bad things going on, and yet we've been given this beautiful afternoon."

"I do know how lucky we are," Alair murmured.

Each of them silently added to themselves, *It's as if the war did not exist.*

Luc rose from the grass, held out his hand to Alair, and pulled her to her feet, saying, "Let's walk down to the lake. I see some swans, and I'd like to see them closer."

All right," she said, and together they walked down the hill.

Still holding her hand, Luc looked down at her. Meeting his gaze, Alair was suddenly aware of the feel of his palm against hers. An excited little thrum of her heart made her feel breathless, and grasping for something to say, she blurted out, "Did you know that all the swans in England belong to the Royal Family?" Once the words were out of her mouth, Alair thought, *What a stupid remark to have made.*

But Luc merely answered seriously, "No. There's a lot about England I don't know. But I'd like to learn."

They were at the lake now, standing under an old elm tree, watching the swans glide over the water in a seemingly effortless way, hardly rippling its surface. It was so still, Alair could almost hear herself breathe. From behind them, where the others were still on the grassy knoll, the sound of voices and laughter floated down to them as if from a long distance away. Luc glanced over his shoulder, then put his arm around Alair's shoulder and drew her to him. She turned, looked up at him, and he leaned to kiss her. Alair stepped back and Luc was instantly apologetic. "I'm sorry, I shouldn't even have tried," he said. "But you looked so beautiful, so—"

"It's just that . . . we hardly know each other."

"Don't we? I guess you're right; it's just that I had the feeling we'd known each other a long time and that—"

Just then they heard their names called and turned to see Cilla and two of the airmen heading in their direction. Cilla held up a paper bag.

"Leftover bread. Crumbs to feed the swans."

Whatever more Luc might have said was gone now, and Alair felt sad that somehow she had missed something important, that a special moment had passed and might never come again.

However, she did know it was a day she would always remember.

It was late in the afternoon by the time they packed up the picnic things and reluctantly left the lovely site and returned to the house.

As soon as they got back, Alair hurried upstairs, bathed and changed, and came downstairs earlier than Cilla, hoping that somehow she might have time alone with Luc. She felt shy, fluttery, not at all herself, remembering the almost kiss under the ancient elm by the lake. She had been down there many times in the past, had examined the bark scarred with dozens of entwined hearts carved with initials, and had often wondered, Who was JM and FD? And did TW truly love BF? And where were all those lovers now? She went into the library, walked over to the window, and looked out at the garden. A purple dusk was falling, and everything looked incredibly beautiful, softened and touched with violet twilight.

Alair felt rather than saw Luc come into the room. But as she slowly turned and saw him coming toward her, she felt a tightening under her heart. What on earth was happening to her? For a moment they simply looked at each other. A line from a poem she had once copied into her scrapbook ran through Alair's mind. It came and went so swiftly, she could not quite recall the words or why it was important. . . .

The moment did not last. With a burst of laughter a group

of couples came into the library, and the room was filled with people. The usual group of young airmen had invaded Birchfields. The room came alive with the sound of voices, laughter, singing, and dance music. Some of Alair's and Cilla's girlfriends had returned, bringing other girls with them from the village, to provide dance partners, serve refreshments, and add to the lighthearted fun.

Frightened by the intensity of her feelings, Alair murmured some excuse and hurried into the dining room, where the punch bowl and platters of sandwiches and cookies had been spread out. For the rest of the evening she kept herself busy, serving, chatting, gaily going from one dance partner to the other. Out of the corner of her eye she occasionally saw Luc. He wasn't dancing. He was watching her. When their gazes met, he smiled but did not tag the shoulder of any of her partners in order to dance with her. Alair was both relieved and bewildered. Still, she felt too unsure of what she was experiencing not to be afraid it would show.

Garnet only stayed long enough to greet some of the newcomers, welcome them to her home, display the charm she had used all her life to make guests feel comfortable and at ease. But she tired soon these days and, leaving the hostessing to the younger women, made her way upstairs, the sounds of congeniality following her.

In a way, this wartime scene brought back her memories of the hectic gaiety of Richmond at the height of the War between the States. Even when they began to realize they were fighting a lost cause, the gallant Confederates danced and sang the nights away. It was somewhat the same now in England. Even though parts of London were burning from the German air raids, at times people still needed to laugh and be happy.

Dance music wafted upstairs to Garnet's room. She had left her door open to listen. The songs, the lyrics, were all different from the ones she remembered. But so much was the same about the evening—pretty young girls dancing with uniformed young men, trying to be happy, forgetting for this one evening what they would soon have to face again. Gradually she began to sway to the melody, then to dance . . . round and round, slowly turning in the pattern the moonlight cast through the windows, humming softly. . . . Once she had waltzed and spun to music, once she had been in love with life and romance, once she had been young . . .

It wasn't until after midnight, when many of the servicemen had returned to the base to make curfew, that Alair and Luc had a chance to be together. Three of Cilla's friends, Sara and Anne Aldrich and Betsy Crane, were going to stay overnight, and when they had seen the last busload leave for the airfield, they all gathered in the library to have a snack and to finish the punch.

"My feet are killing me!" wailed Cilla, sitting down and kicking off her pumps and wriggling her toes.

"That's what you get for being the belle of the ball," Luc teased. "I didn't see you sit down all evening."

"I know. But some of those fellows need dancing lessons." She rubbed her stocking toes with a pained expression.

"Good idea. Why don't you give them?"

"I feel like I did tonight," she retorted.

"Listen, everyone, I need your help," Alair said and everyone turned to her. "About the fund-raising fete Mama and Aunt Lalage are giving at Blanding Court—I have an idea for the program. Since it's going to be on April twenty-third, I thought we'd have a pantomime and have people guess the theme, and the one who gets it right will win a prize. That way the children can all be in it. They can be villagers—they'd love screaming with fright and running about."

"We'll have to make costumes, of course," said Sarah.

"That won't be a problem," countered Alair.

"Except for the dragon. That will be a real job. What could we use for his scales?"

"Paper mache?"

Everyone leaped in with suggestions until finally Luc tapped on his punch cup with a spoon and held up one hand, saying, "At the risk of being nominated as some kind of idiot, will someone please tell me what this is all about?"

A moment of dead silence followed. Luc looked around from one blank face to the next, then said, "From the way everyone is staring at me, I've exposed my ignorance to a monumental degree, and no one is going to enlighten me. Am I the only one who doesn't know what any of this has to do with April twenty-third?"

"Saint George's Day, of course!" came all of the voices in unison.

"Who is Saint George, and why does he have a day?"

Cilla looked at him with mock disbelief. "Surely, even in America you've heard of Saint George and the dragon, Luc?"

Luc glanced at Alair. "Want to explain?"

"Of course," she said sympathetically. "It's an old legend that goes back hundreds of years, but every English schoolchild knows it. It's the story of the rescue of the beautiful daughter of the King of Silene in the third century, when she was chosen to be the appeasement of a terrible dragon who was terrorizing the countryside, devouring people. That's when Saint George came in, the veritable shining knight on a white charger, to save the damsel in distress. April twenty-third is the day he's remembered and honored, and there are celebrations, fetes, parades, and all sorts of things."

"I just had another terrific idea!" Cilla exclaimed, almost jumping up. "Luc would make a perfect Saint George, and you, Alair, can be the princess."

Luc's eyes twinkled as he looked at Alair. "Done. I'd be happy to rescue Alair any day, to say nothing of April twenty-third."

The discussion of the staging, the costumes, the scenery, needed for the program continued enthusiastically until yawns and drooping eyelids finally put a stop to the planning. Cilla and the other three girls left to go upstairs. But at the bottom of the stairway Luc and Alair lingered.

"It's been a wonderful day," he said. "I hate to think of going back tomorrow."

"But you will be here for the rehearsals and the fete on the twenty-third?" she said anxiously.

"Yes. If I'm not flying."

At his words reality struck. As lovely as this weekend was for Alair—meeting Luc, spending time with him, getting to know him—it was all tentative. Plans could not really be made. He had a higher priority than playing the role of Saint George in a children's pantomime. No matter that she and Luc were young and perhaps on the brink of falling in love—this was wartime, and they could not escape the dark cloud hovering over them.

As luck would have it—or rather, because Luc had offered to trade flights with another pilot in his squadron—Luc was at Blanding Court on April twenty-third. He got there in time to don a paper suit of armor, mount a stick horse, and wield a broom handle spear at a monstrous creature, made of yards of bilious-green-colored paper cut in jagged shapes, with ferocious horns and teeth. Alair was a fairy-tale princess, with a chiffon scarf floating from a cardboard crown, and the children were appropriately terrified as they scampered all over, emitting shouts and yells that ended in hilarious giggles, before the dragon was properly slain and the curtain pulled shut. The fund-raising itself was very successful, and the evening party continued the celebration. Alair changed from her princess costume into an azure dress that deepened her cornflower blue eyes. Luc was waiting for her when she came downstairs.

From the drawing room came the faint sound of the local band tuning up to play for the evening's dancing. The melody of a familiar and very popular song began softly playing.

"Good evening, Princess," he greeted her softly.

"Why, if it isn't Saint George," she said, smiling.

Luc held out both hands and asked, "Shall we dance?" She went into his arms and they moved slowly to the melody. "I'll be seeing you in all the old familiar places . . . ," the vocalist sang plaintively. The words had just that tiny hint of optimism that all the war songs *had* to have, the hope that some lucky few would come through all this, would be together again. One had to dream, one had to hope, one had to pray, that you and the one you loved would be among them.

Afterward Alair could never remember how long they danced or how often Luc had requested the band to play that number. How many dances, Alair lost count. She had lost awareness of anyone or anything else. She had not even noticed her mother's frequent glances at her and Luc. She lost track of time until Luc's arm around her waist tightened and he leaned closer and whispered, "I don't want this evening to end."

"I don't either," she sighed.

"I wish it could go on and on. I don't want to go back to the base. I don't want to leave you."

Alair did not know what to reply. What she was feeling was new, hard to explain even to herself. Luc drew her closer. "This is our song. I'll never hear it without thinking of you." He began to sing in a low voice, "I'll be seeing you . . . in everything that's light and gay, I'll always think of you that way."

As she listened to Luc sing the words, Alair knew she would never forget this night as long as she lived. Luc had found a place in her heart that had been unfilled until now, and made it his. It would never belong to anyone else. No matter what happened.

It was getting late, and they would have to say good-bye. In a few more hours Luc would have to return to the base, report to his barracks. In the morning he would get his briefing and assignment.

Lady Blanding was at the door saying good night to the last guests when Luc was ready to leave. He looked at Alair, longing to kiss the soft mouth, to hold her, tell her that he had fallen in love with her, that he believed they were meant for each other. But of course he couldn't, not with her mother and all these other strangers present. Luc hesitated. Maybe it was too soon. Maybe she didn't feel the same way he did. He reached out and took her hand. She laced her fingers into his and looked up at him. In that heart-stopping moment he saw in her eyes the possibility that they shared a dream of love.

His letter was delivered to Blanding Court two days later. As she took it out of the envelope, she thought he must have written it as soon as he got back to his barracks. His opening told her she had been right.

My darling Alair,

I hope I can say that, because it's the way I think of you. However, I must ask myself if I have the right to say "my." So I'll start again. . . . Darling Alair, I'm sitting on the edge of my bunk, writing this by flashlight—or "torch," as you Brits would say. My buddies have long since gone to sleep. I find myself wide-awake, yet I seem to be dreaming. Could it have happened? Could all of it really have happened? To meet someone for the first time and feel as though you have known that person all your life somehow. I know all the wise, cautious, sane things people say about wartime romances. But I think there are exceptions. I hope you think so, too. It was almost as though it were not our first meeting. Of course, we had heard about each other most of our lives, through all the family connections, so maybe we each had some foreknowledge that the other existed. However, I believe it was more than that. . . . Do you know the poem "Fate"?

> *Two shall be born the whole wide world apart,*
> *And speak in different tongues,*
> *And then o'er unknown lands to unknown seas shall cross,*
> *Escaping wreck, defying death,*
> *And all unconsciously*
> *Shape every working thought and every wandering step,*
> *To this one end—that one day out of darkness,*
> *They may meet, and read life's meaning in each other's eyes.*

Alair drew in her breath. Her hands holding the letter began to shake. It was the same poem from which the last line had fleetingly come into her mind that first evening. It must be significant. It must mean something more than ordinary coincidence.

She went back to his letter.

I didn't quote the second stanza, because it is too terrible. If you remember, it was about two people who didn't meet, although they should have. How often the course of our lives is determined by chance. I believe we are the lucky ones. I thank God for our meeting.

I shall try to wrangle leave for next weekend—that is, if you are free and can see me. You never know here how things will go. But if I can possibly be there, I will come. It would mean everything to me if we could spend some time together.

> *Yours,*
> *Luc Montrose*

chapter
19

WHEN NIKI ROUTINELY CHECKED her mailbox and found the manila folder containing orders to report to Colonel Thornton's London office the next day, she was amazed. In the weeks since her interview, she had resigned herself to the fact that she was not going to be called for any kind of special assignment.

She was both excited and apprehensive. This was what she wanted, wasn't it? Yes, but that was before she and Fraser . . .

Quickly she thrust those thoughts aside. This was wartime. If there was anything she could do to free her beloved France or help in any way the effort to defeat the Nazis, no personal consideration mattered.

If Fraser were ordered to some special duty, he would not hesitate.

Niki ran up the steps to her cabin, two at a time. She would have to catch the next train to London. There was hardly enough time to do anything but pack, make a few phone calls.

Her heart was beating so fast, she could hardly breathe. At last something was happening. A new kind of challenge. As Tante used to say at the start of any new phase in life, "Think of it as a great adventure."

Colonel Thornton looked up as she was ushered into his office. Niki saluted and he gestured to a chair opposite his desk.

Briefly he told her that her application had been reviewed and in light of her bilingual skills, she was being assigned to a special training unit. She would be issued a travel warrant from London to Scotland, where she would be met at . . . He wrote the name of the town on a slip of paper, handed it to her, saying tersely, "Top secret. Read it, memorize it, tear it up."

Niki felt a chill, like a cold finger trailing down the back of her neck. She'd asked for something like this. But after nothing had come of her first interview, she had given up hope that she would ever be called. Colonel Thornton gave her a hard look from under his bushy eyebrows.

"You haven't changed your mind, have you?" he demanded.

"No sir," she said quickly.

"Good. You understand it is absolutely essential that you discuss this with no one. Not even your closest friend, your family." He frowned. "Or boyfriend. Do you have a boyfriend?"

The thought of Fraser flashed through her mind, and Niki pushed it away. She couldn't call him a boyfriend after only four meetings, could she?

"No sir."

"Good. That's all, then. The date and time of your train is on this." Another slip of paper was passed over to her. Then Colonel Thornton stood up, saying, "Good luck." He saluted her.

Niki got to her feet, saluted, and walked out of the office, the slip of paper that was going to change her life clutched tightly in her hand.

Niki stepped off the train at the bleak Loch Ennis station and was immediately chilled by the cold, damp wind. She felt stiff and achy from the long trip north to Scotland, as well as apprehensive as to what lay ahead.

It had been a tense time. Elly of course had been curious, but all Niki could tell her was that she'd been tapped for some special training. She told the same story to Bryanne when she called Birchfields. She had tried to reach Fraser but had only been able to leave a message. The voice that had answered at his base said only that he wasn't available and that he would put her message in his box. Niki hated leaving without talking to him. But she couldn't have told him anything anyway. Maybe it was better not to clutter up her resolve but to be totally committed to whatever this new assignment involved. She knew their attraction for each other was strong and could make her less willing to take on whatever it was.

Niki straightened her jacket, her hat, knowing that her uniform—which had been neatly pressed, her shirt fresh, when she boarded the train yesterday—was now rumpled and looked as though it had been slept in, which it had.

There were six people standing in a group at the other end of the nearly empty platform, one officer, four men in army fatigues, and one woman in the uniform of the army nurse corps. Since there was nobody else about, Niki decided this must be the rest of the team she'd be joining. She shouldered her overarm bag and walked slowly over to them. She smiled and tried to make eye contact, but most of them did not respond. Everyone stood, shoulders hunched, obviously trying to brace themselves against the cutting wind.

The officer, a stern-faced man, approached. "I'm Captain Mullen," he announced and went down the line, shaking hands, the four men first, then the nurse, and finally Niki. She started to say, "I'm Wren Gilbreaux" when he snapped, "Name not necessary."

Rebuked, Niki blushed hotly.

"We'll be boarding the bus now," the officer barked. "Briefing then."

As they lined up to get on the gray-brown camouflaged bus, the army nurse whispered, "I guess this is going to be bare knuckles, no Marquess of Queensbury rules." Niki gave her a grateful smile, glad that someone in this crowd had a sense of humor.

It was a jolting, rough journey until they finally arrived at a bleak stone building. It looked as though it might be the kind of boarding school to which Charlotte Bronte's Jane Eyre had been sent to, Niki thought with some amusement. But that was about the last amusing thought Niki was to have in several long weeks.

At Loch Ennis their day began at five. A stand-up breakfast of bread, tea or coffee, was followed by a two-mile walk whatever the weather. Scotland at this time of year seemed terminally overcast or raining. After this came an hour's calisthenics. The midday meal consisted of a nondescript soup, more bread, rice pudding or junket. In the afternoons there where lectures—some on the geography of France, others on how to identify various kinds of German aircraft by learning the parts from fuselage to tail. Niki had never been the least bit interested in mechanics, so she found it hard to remain alert and attentive during these hours. Harder still for a girl like her with no mechanical ability were the radio labs. Here they were given the components of small transmitter radios, told to construct one from the instructions, then take it apart, put it together again. Niki felt hopelessly clumsy at this. Before the day ended, another hour was spent in a saturation course in phonetic French. Of course, this was easier for her. In this she could help Jennifer and Max, the two members of the team with whom she had become friends. It was hard to make real friends during such intense indoctrination. The fact that everyone was so focused on making the grade created an unnatural atmosphere, not one conducive to easy friendship. Evenings were supposed to be more relaxed, but actually most everyone was worn out from the long day of physical and mental effort. People tended to make it a short evening, with few lingering in the huge lounge after dinner.

Some nights Jennifer would knock on Niki's door and come in for a brief chat. Niki could tell that in spite of how arduous her nurse's training might have been, Jennifer found this hard going. Niki sensed her nervousness and sympathized. But neither of them allowed themselves to confess their fears or their doubts. It was as if expressing them would make them too real. All they wanted was to qualify for whatever the point of the training was. Rumors were rife, but no one knew exactly what their mission would be. Were they to be couriers, agents, radio operators? All they knew was that they were being closely monitored to determine the category for which they would best be fitted.

The morning after their first rock climbing exercise on the cliffs above the stormy ocean, one of the team was missing. No one asked why. He had had an obvious emotional problem about heights. As they were climbing, linked by a rope, he had frozen, unable to go up or down. Both those above him and those below him were stuck in their positions by his immobility. Eventually he pulled it together and made it to the top. But there he was shaking so visibly that it was impossible for him to hide it from the others. The next morning he didn't show up. Nothing was explained. But it was clear to the rest that there were no second chances. The experience troubled Niki deeply. She had been scared silly herself but somehow had managed this climb. Still, there were two more climbs ahead, each progressively more difficult.

The morning of the second climb, Niki tried not to think of what had happened to her teammate. When they hiked to the bottom of the rock cliff, she did not dare look up to the top. There was nothing to do but clench her jaw, grit her teeth, and begin. Look for the first handhold, grip it, search for a toe-hold, move steadily upward, keep climbing. "Nice view," Max quipped from behind her, but Niki only clamped her teeth together harder and reached for the next crevice. Only sheer grit kept her going.

The days passed until they'd been there three weeks—the halfway point. There were still five of them. They knew the final physical trial was coming, a survival test. The morning it was scheduled, Niki woke up with a stomachache. Nerves, she told herself. She managed to swallow some tea, a crust of bread. They were issued a compass, a basic ration pack, a tarpaulin folded into an oilskin envelope. They piled into a van and were driven out to a stretch of moor at least thirty miles from the building. There they were told to report back in twenty-four hours.

Niki knew this was the ultimate physical test. The make-or-break one. If, as the teammates had discussed among themselves, they were to parachute into occupied France, they would be on their own, have to manage on minimum supplies, having been given a map to get to the nearest "safe house." There, presumably, a member of the French Resistance would help them until they set up the shortwave radio in the designated place. So this was the test to see if they could pass muster. It was a preview of what they'd face on a mission. They'd either pass or be sent away.

Niki was determined. She'd come this far, and she was grimly committed to making it. Captain Mullen had been particularly hard on her and Jennifer. Privately they thought that his discriminatory attitude toward them was because he didn't think women should be recruited for this kind of duty. He almost expected them to fail. That made Niki doubly resolved.

The weather that morning was beastly. The wind was sharp as a steel knife, penetrating even through their parkas and wool caps. Then it began to rain. The wind increased, driving the icy rain against them as they struggled to find their way back across the desolate stretch of stubbled grassland. Moors provided very little possibility of shelter. When the rain began to come down in sheets, they huddled together next to a large boulder, spreading the tarp over themselves.

I've never been this cold in my life, Niki thought, shuddering, her teeth chattering. *I wish I were anywhere else but here. Why did I think I wanted this?*

The other four were just as miserable, but Max managed a joke. He told them this reminded him of the time he'd gone to Wimbledon to see the tennis matches. He'd dressed to the nines, in white flannels, new shoes, and a new straw hat, when he'd been caught between the courts in a downpour. It wasn't that funny, but they needed some comic relief, and they all laughed heartily.

Niki was never sure how, but the team did manage to straggle back to the building twenty minutes before the deadline. Bedraggled, soaked, bone weary, and bleary-eyed with lack of sleep, she barely remembered staggering upstairs, into a hot bath, then to sleep.

The next morning they came down to a breakfast the likes of which they had not seen here before. Platters of sausage, eggs, cinnamon rolls, fried apples, were set out for them. Best of all, Captain Mullen congratulated them on their accomplishment.

That afternoon a rumor circulated regarding the arrival of some top brass. This meant the team would have to appear for an oral interview, which would result in an evaluation that would be the final hurdle, determine if they would make the cut.

Jennifer and Niki waited their turn, talking in whispers in the lounge while the three men were being interviewed.

Adding up all the various elements in their training, they were convinced that passing this last test would mean being secreted into occupied France to carry out a mission.

In her mind Niki went over her chances. She knew she had passed the physical tests successfully, had done fairly well on some of the others parts of the training, such as map reading and airplane recognition, but had been weak on the mechanical stuff. Her one sure advantage was her fluency in French, however.

"Gilbreaux." The sound of her name snapped her to attention. She stood up, straightened her uniform jacket, and walked into the interview room.

Niki tried to stay calm, give clear, concise answers to the questions they asked. One of the officers launched into a rapid flow of French. Niki made a quick switch from English and was able to understand and reply to all that he said. He gave a brief nod, and the other officers exchanged looks that she interpreted as approving.

When it was over, she was told she had a three-day leave during which she could make her final decision as to whether she wanted to be included in the mission her team would be assigned.

"But I can answer that right now. Yes, of course."

Jennifer was waiting for her and they hugged each other, relieved that they had both made the cut. Since Niki had discovered that Jennifer had no immediate family and her boyfriend was in North Africa, and because Niki decided it would be too difficult to go to Birchfields and keep the secret of her new assignment, they decided to spend their leave together at a nice Scottish inn they'd heard about.

Niki felt sad not to see Garnet and Bryanne, but she thought the dear old lady would have a fit if she knew what she was about to do. She didn't dare tell Luc either. He still had his image of her as irresponsible, flighty, self-centered. She must prove herself a grown-up, capable person, someone he could be proud of. She thought of calling Fraser but decided against that too. It would just complicate things between them. *When I get back, I'll confide in him,* Niki promised herself. She didn't listen to a small voice inside that suggested she should change that *when* to an *if.*

One question she had been asked during the final interview bothered her now a great deal. It had been put to her by Colonel Thornton: "You will be issued a suicide pill before embarking to France. Do you have any religious scruples about taking it in the event you are captured?"

She had been so anxious to make the grade, to be considered the right stuff for this dangerous work, that she had answered without hesitation. "No sir."

But that night she lay sleepless, knowing that it wasn't true. She hated the thought of being tortured, but ending her own life? It would never come to that, she tried to reassure herself. Still, that haunting thought hovered when she woke up the next morning. It was too late to recant. She was in this for the long haul. The small band of interrogating officers had left, and all the others were embarking on their short final leave. She would just have to rely on her new faith, her trust in God to keep her safe, bring her through whatever happened.

chapter

20

WHEN NIKI AND JENNIFER returned from their three-day leave, they were told to report to the airfield the next morning. The team was being flown to Gibraltar. There one of the leaders of the French underground would arrive to take charge of their crossing into occupied France.

In Gibraltar they were housed in a large seaside villa for two days.

During the afternoon of the second day Niki and Jennifer were sunbathing. Hot and thirsty, Niki offered to go inside and bring them back something cool to drink. On her way into the house, she happened to glance back at the terraced garden that led down to the beach. She halted, stood absolutely still as she watched a man climbing up the rocky steps. Behind him on the crescent of sand a boat had been beached. As she watched him come, a ripple of shock went through her. The shape of the head, the set of the shoulders, were familiar. She stiffened. She was sure. It was Paul Duval.

He was wearing a beret and a rough workman's smock of blue cotton. He continued up the rock steps bordered with flame red geraniums. Although he was not aware of her, she could see his face. It was tense. His mouth was a thin line, a cigarette dangling from one end. His eyes were squinted against the glare of the sun, so he didn't see her. Niki felt a rush of blood tingling through her body. She felt hot, then cold, in spite of the sun's warmth on her bare back and arms. Paul, here. There could be no other reason than that he was the Resistance leader who would take their team into France.

As she stood there, half hidden from sight by one of the marble pillars of the terrace, Niki saw Captain Mullen, their training officer, hurry down the steps to greet Paul. The two men stood talking for a few minutes. Then they both walked rapidly into the house, unaware they had been observed.

Niki, shaken by what she had seen, went back to where Jennifer was still drowsing in the sun. She confided eagerly what she had seen and what it likely meant. "Then we'll probably be going in the morning," Jennifer said excitedly.

Just then Max came to tell them that they were to report to the drawing room of the mansion for a briefing at four o'clock. Eagerly he and Jennifer discussed the reason for the meeting. Niki was strangely silent. She had an uneasy feeling. She both looked forward to and dreaded seeing Paul.

Why, she wasn't quite sure. Paul, of all people, would understand her motivation to do something to help her native country. But somehow as it approached four o'clock, Niki felt very apprehensive.

Her premonition proved right. Paul visibly paled, looked shocked, when he saw her among the group gathered for the briefing. He gave no indication that he knew her but, after being introduced to the team by Captain Mullen, proceeded to tell them about the operation. They would go by boat, the one he himself had brought to the island and left waiting on the beach below. They would be met on the other side by a group of fishermen, who were loyal Resistance members. From there they would get further orders where to go, what to do.

There was a short period for questions, but there were only

a few. Captain Mullen closed the meeting by saying that clothing, supplies, would be delivered to each person's room later. They were to be dressed as peasants so they would not stand out in any way in the small village where they would land.

By ten o'clock that night no one had come to Niki's door with the issue of clothes and supplies. The inner dread slowly became a reality. For some reason she had been scratched from the team.

By whom and why, she was to learn.

Finally there came a knock at her door. She had been sitting on the edge of her bed in a tense waiting position for hours. Now she ran to open it and found Paul standing there.

"May I come in?"

"Of course."

Neither said any of the things that friends meeting after a long time would be expected to say.

Niki was stiff with apprehension, Paul obviously agitated. He took a pack of cigarettes from his shirt pocket, shook one out, looked at her, raised his eyebrow and asked, "Mind?"

She shook her head. He was nervous, she could tell. She almost knew what he was going to say and also that he hated saying it. She felt sorry for him. But she wasn't going to help him. He had to tell her himself.

"You've been removed from the mission tomorrow."

"I can't be," she said numbly, even though she had expected it.

"Sorry. It's been decided."

"Who decided? Captain Mullen? You?"

Paul dragged on his cigarette. "It doesn't matter. It was decided." He paused. "But if you insist on knowing, yes, it's my job to select the right people, weed out the unfit, the ones who could sabotage the operation, because any weak link endangers the entire chain. That's my responsibility."

"It's not fair." She hated that her voice sounded girlish, whining. Quickly she gathered her composure. Acting childish wouldn't help her cause. "Do I get an explanation?"

"No, you just follow orders," he replied shortly. "You're to return to England. You'll get a new assignment there."

Niki's disappointment, chagrin, was hard to control. Her hands clenched at her sides. Should she plead, argue, beg? Would it do any good? Paul looked around for an ashtray, found none, and Niki automatically pushed the saucer of an empty teacup she'd left on the dresser toward him. He crushed out his half-smoked cigarette, then turned to her, saying, "Any questions?"

"I've been trained to not ask questions, just obey orders." Her tone was bitter. "But yes, of course I have questions. Can we speak one to one, friend to friend?"

"Go ahead."

"What is the real reason I'm being removed? I passed all the tests, qualified. Besides, I speak fluent French. No one else on the team speaks it as well. Can you afford to keep me from going?"

Paul started pacing, hands clasped behind his back, his face like granite. "That's not the point."

"Then what is the point? I don't understand."

Paul halted, stood at the window, his back toward her.

"Why me, why now? It's personal, isn't it? Paul, answer me."

He whirled around, facing her. "Yes! If anything happened to you, how could I face Luc? Or your parents?" His eyes narrowed. "Do you know what could happen to you if you were captured? What do you think the cyanide pills they issue you are for? Men stronger than you have cracked under Nazi torture. What makes you think you wouldn't?" Paul's eyes blazed. "Could you do it, Niki, if it came to that? Take your own life?"

His question hung between them as he continued to confront her with an unflinching stare.

For a minute Niki was silent. She had answered the question in the interview, but Paul's eyes seemed to probe her inmost soul. Could she? Her life was only half lived. There were so many things she wanted to do, to accomplish. In her mind's eye were images of the people she loved and might never see again—Tante, Uncle Kip, Luc. Never to see Montclair again. And Fraser. All the possibilities of loving him floated before her. Never to deeply love or marry, have children. To die not knowing any of these things. Would she have the courage? To end her life, God's gift to her? But on the other hand, could she trust herself not to break?

"Niki?" Paul's voice broke into her troubling thoughts.

He was waiting for some kind of response. Was he really giving her a choice, or was his word final? She thought of that day in Saint Paul's when she had stood in front of the painting *The Light of the World* and resolved to open the door of her heart, to surrender her life to God. Was Paul's decision God's way of showing her what she was supposed to do? A good soldier followed orders.

She looked at Paul and saw beyond the hardened commander, the man who had seen terrible things, to the dashing young man with a mischievous smile, dark, dancing eyes, lighthearted humor. It made her heart wrench to see only a shadow of the Paul she had known. He was changed, as she was changed. The war had changed everyone.

Paul must have read her thoughts, for his expression softened slightly.

"You've proved enough, Niki. Be proud of what you've done. There are other ways you can serve. Your ability as a translator would be invaluable. I'll recommend you. As for now, your orders are to return to England. You'll get a new assignment there." Paul hesitated a little longer. "So, Niki, can we part still friends?"

She didn't answer but turned away, unable to hold back the tears she did not want him to see. What if he was right? Maybe she wasn't strong enough. Had all this difficult training been wasted?

"Au revoir," Paul said gently.

She did not know he was gone, until she heard the firm click of the door closing.

Disheartened, depressed, Niki returned to WRENS head-quarters, to her old job. Two weeks passed. The promised new assignment never materialized. She had no way of checking to find out why. Had the team completed the operation safely? Had anything happened to them? What about Paul? Had he forgotten? Or was he unable to fulfill his promise?

Then Fraser called to tell her that he had a weekend pass. The following day, as they sat in the small cafe where they'd gone after the cinema, Niki told him as much as she felt she could without bridging security.

"I wanted it so badly. I worked so hard. And then at the last minute—" She shook her head, all the old disappointment coming to the surface.

"I take it that it was a risky venture, something dangerous?"

"You might say that. But I was prepared," she protested. "And after all, it was for the war effort, for France, my country."

Fraser reached over, took her hand, and said gently, "Maybe it wasn't in God's plan for your life, Niki. Have you considered that?"

She looked at him, wide-eyed. They had never spoken of spiritual things. Now as she looked at him, his candid eyes full of caring and concern, she felt a strong bonding. Here was a man she could trust, a man she could love.

"Yes," she replied slowly. "Maybe you're right."

"I believe that nothing in life happens by chance, Niki," he said.

Sunday evening, before he left to go back to his base, he said, "Listen, Niki, I'm about due for a week's leave. I want to take you to Kingaren. I want my mum to meet you, and you to meet her and my younger sister Fiona. They'll tell you all sorts of wild tales about me, and mum will want to show you my baby pictures. You'll suffer, I promise you, but on the other hand," he added, grinning, "you'd have to find all this out sooner or later if—"

"If what?" Niki teased.

"You're foolish enough to marry me."

"You haven't asked me to."

"What would you say if I did?"

"I don't know. I'll have to hear all those wild tales and see those baby pictures, I guess."

Fraser laughed. "You're on. Start working on getting at least four days off. Trade with someone or take extra duty. I've already alerted mum, and she'll be writing you a formal invitation. That's to comply with all that protocol your proper Southern upbringing expects."

Fraser was always gently ribbing her about being a Virginian and growing up on a plantation.

"It's *your* family's plantation, not mine!" she would declare, feigning indignation.

"It's your brother Luc who will inherit Montclair, be master there. I've always known that. Besides, after the war I'll go happily back to Scotland, find a crofter's cottage I can restore, put in plumbing and all that modern stuff for my American bride, then spend my days fishing."

"You're taking a lot for granted, aren't you, you arrogant Scot?"

"Well, what else can I do? What can any of us do but dream of the future?" His face was suddenly sober. "The present's too ugly." That was a rare break for Fraser. They hardly ever talked about the war, discussed its progress, confessed their anxieties. Time together was too precious.

chapter
21

Birchfields

EVERYONE SEEMED SURPRISED when Alair and Luc announced they wanted to be married, although Garnet had a secret smile, as though she had been the only one in on the secret. Hadn't she seen it from the first, their immediate attraction to each other that day Luc arrived at Birchfields? It was so obvious; how could no one else have noticed? Garnet offered Birchfields for the reception. It was closer to the village church where the wedding was going to be than Blanding Court was, and therefore much more convenient in these times when transportation was so difficult. She did not mention the fact that for her, traveling to Blanding Court to attend would involve a great deal of trouble. Lalage agreed and gratefully accepted, since Neil was in London, deeply involved in his work at the War Office, and Blanding Court was crowded with all its evacuees. Alair and Luc wanted a small country wedding, just family and a few friends. While Lady Blanding and her sister Lenora Ridgeway busied themselves with preparations, Luc started the process of getting leave for a honeymoon, which turned out to be only four days. Pilots of Luc's experience and skill were too valuable to be off duty for long.

Only Niki seemed left out of the planning. She was amazed and chagrined at her own reaction to the romance. She had not been at Birchfields the week Luc and Alair had met, so the whirlwind romance had caught her completely by surprise. The fact that Luc—her darling, special Luc—was head over heels in love with Alair Blanding had come as a shock. Why it should have, she knew, was outrageous on her part. Alair was beautiful, gentle, refined, and Luc, a romantic, would have of course fallen for her ethereal looks, her soft voice and gentle manner. Aunt Garnet reported to Niki that she had never seen two people more in love.

Why didn't she feel happy about the announcement? Didn't all the world love a lover? Wasn't it a sign of hope that such a lovely thing could happen in a world now torn with hate and tragedy? What was wrong with her?

She had long ago given up on the preposterous idea that *she* could marry Luc. When she was a little girl, she had dreamed that when they grew up they would marry and live forever at Montclair, raising horses and riding through the autumn woods together. Certainly, now she had put that fantasy away with other childish dreams. *Hadn't* she?

Niki was ashamed at her reaction. How stupid and immature to be jealous of something she had no right to anyway. Still, her heart ached, because she knew that Luc's new love would supersede anything they had together. That's the way it was. That's what was written in the marriage ceremony: "Henceforth you shall leave father, mother, and cleave only unto the other. . . ." In a way, she was losing Luc, and that's what hurt. Of course, she was not losing him entirely but in the special way she had always had him.

Niki told herself she had to get over these troublesome feelings. Since the wedding was going to be a simple one, not the lavish social affair that Alair's father—being a lord, a member of Parliament, and now a major in the military—might have demanded if not for the war, Niki was not included in the wedding party. Alair was only having her cousin Cilla as her single attendant. The fact that Luc was marrying someone from an aristocratic family removed him further from Niki. The Blanding family went back for centuries. They knew the names of all their ancestors, while Niki didn't know who she was or where she came from. For the first time in a long while, the ache of not knowing surfaced. The old hurt, the loneliness of not really belonging, swept over Niki.

The fact that she couldn't share these feelings with anyone made it even worse. Keeping it to herself haunted her troubled heart. She sincerely wished Luc happiness. Alair did not need her wishes, she thought with a twinge. She had Luc; what other happiness did she need?

Niki got a two-day pass and arrived in the village by an early train the morning of the wedding. There was no time to go up to Birchfields and change out of her WRENS uniform, so she walked through the morning mist to the small, stone church and slipped into one of the back pews. This church was hundreds of years old, and even the fragrance of the flowers now banking the altar steps could not completely shut out the odor of damp old stones, the ancient scent of the wax candles that had been burned here for centuries.

It was the first war wedding to be held here, perhaps because the small village was largely inhabited by older people living in the few large homes. Until the recent building of the airfield, there had been few young people to even attend Sunday services. Soon Niki became aware of a subdued ripple of voices reverberating through the cold church. She turned in time to see the arrival of a small contingent of young girls. They were in school uniforms, so she guessed they were from the nearby academy and had slipped into the chapel. Giggling a little, their eyes bright with excitement, their heads full of romantic fantasy, they settled like a flock of nervous starlings into another of the back pews, opposite the one Niki was occupying. She smiled, imagining they were all wishing they were a few years older so they could be part of all the excitement that the young men in uniform had brought to the streets of their usually quiet town. Had they skipped class to come, Niki wondered, or had some school holiday left them free to attend?

The stir of activity in the vestibule alerted Niki that the bridal party had probably arrived. The bride's mother, Lady Blanding, dressed in royal blue, a silver fox fur draped across her slim shoulders, and accompanied by her sister, Mrs. Victor Ridgeway, arrived first. They were escorted down the aisle by two handsome young officers. New friends of Luc's from his outfit, Niki assumed, again feeling the little prick of alienation. She used to know *all* of Luc's friends. He brought them home in droves from Briarwood Prep and college. Except for the one leave they had spent together in London, they had not seen much of each other. Of course, it was wartime and they both had duties; it couldn't be helped. But now Niki wished she'd made more of an effort to coordinate her time off with his. She was always welcome at Birchfields, she knew, but simply had not come as often as she could have.

A lady in a strange-looking hat took her place at the organ, and the first chords rumbled through the church. A waft of familiar perfume wrinkled Niki's nose, and she turned her head slightly, just in time to see Aunt Garnet, handsome in russet velvet, wearing a mink stole and turbaned hat, enter on the arm of one of the uniformed ushers. She moved with great dignity, as if for the occasion she had willed away the halting walk her arthritis sometimes caused.

Soon Luc and his best man, a fellow officer, came from the side door and took their place. A few minutes later there was an anticipatory hush, and then the congregation stood as the first notes of "The Wedding March" sounded. Alair, in a mist of veiling and swirls of white silk, carrying a small nosegay of violets, escorted by Lord Blanding in dress uniform, came forward down the aisle. The beautiful ancient ceremony began.

As Niki listened to the couple repeat the age-old vows, looking at each other with such love, she experienced a mixture of envy and hopelessness. Tears she did not want to shed rushed into her eyes. Furiously she blinked them back. She wanted to be happy for Luc and Alair, she really did. But there was a void in her own life, a longing in her heart to know the kind of devotion they expressed.

Somehow she got through the ceremony and through the reception at Birchfields that followed, and with the rest of the family and friends sent Alair and Luc off on their honeymoon. She was grateful she had to report back to WRENS headquarters the next day. For the first time, the dull routine of duty seemed an escape.

Larkspur Cottage, with its thatched roof and diamond-paned windows, was picture perfect. A riot of orange, yellow, russet nasturtiums clambered over a stone wall. Closer to the blue door, a hydrangea bush heavy with blossoms nodded in a gentle breeze.

As he pulled the Austin-mini up front, Luc remarked to Alair, "It's straight out of a storybook."

"It looks like one of those nostalgic nineteenth-century paintings. The ones critics complained romanticized English country life."

"It looks OK to me," Luc laughed, and he jumped out of the car and got their luggage out of the boot. He held open the gate for Alair to go through ahead of him. "Want me to carry you over the threshold?"

"Of course."

He set down their suitcases and lifted her up easily, and they went inside. Aunt Garnet had arranged to have the place aired, cleaned, and it smelled faintly of lemon wax polish. A fire was laid in the fireplace of the cozy sitting room. Luc put Alair down and she turned slowly, looking around. "How lucky we are!" she said, smiling at him.

To begin their married life together in such a place was ideal. Four days of peace, privacy, learning to love each other in an entirely new way. It was as though they were the only two people in the world.

They spent their days like misers, savoring each golden moment yet feeling as though they were grasping time, holding on to it as the days rushed past. They took long walks, talking about all sorts of things—their childhood, their growing-up years, the books they'd read, the music they liked, the people they admired, things they hadn't had time to tell each other about themselves in their brief courtship. They made meals together with much laughter and teasing, finding out about each other's tastes in food, and learning their differences as well as how much they had in common. In the evening, as outside the glen mist surrounded the woodland cottage, shutting them off from the world, they listened to records and danced to favorite tunes, sat in front of the fireplace. They went to sleep in each other's arms and woke up each morning counting themselves blessed to have another day to spend together. They talked about many things, but they did not talk much about the future. The next weekend they could possibly have together was as far into the future as they wanted to discuss or, for that matter, could plan.

On the last day before Luc had to report back to the airfield and Alair to Blanding Court to continue her work with the kindergarten children, they finally spoke of some of the things they had avoided. They spoke of the uncertainty they were facing. It was then that Alair wept, voicing her dread of their separation.

"But we're no different from thousands of other couples," Luc said.

She nodded. "Yes, I know you're right."

"I still feel we're among the lucky ones who are going to get through all this and then have our whole life ahead of us," Luc told her, even as he wiped the tears running down her cheeks.

Luc had already flown seventeen of the twenty-five requisite missions that American pilots had to fly before being sent back to the States for R and R. He hadn't told Alair yet, but when he'd flown the twenty-fifth, he intended to ask that his time off be spent in England.

At last it was time to pack up and leave. On the doorstep Alair said softly, "Maybe we can come back someday—if we're lucky."

Luc smiled at her fondly, proud of her bravery even though he saw the uncertainty in her eyes. He reached out and touched her cool, rose-tinted cheek, aware of how the sun sent glints of gold through her hair. "I love you," he said. Then he locked the door, pocketed the key, and they went out to the car and drove away. Neither had the courage to look back.

chapter

22

TWO WEEKS AFTER Luc and Alair's wedding, Niki received a note from Phoebe Montrose, Fraser's mother. It was written on stationery from the McPherson Arms Hotel, and the handwriting was both strong and refined.

> *Fraser has written so glowingly of your meeting and the gracious hospitality shown him at Mrs. Devlin's country home. I remember it so pleasantly from the time when, as a young woman, I met his father, Jonathan, there. We would be so happy if you were able to arrange to accompany Fraser home sometime soon.*

> *Looking forward to that occasion,*
> *I am yours most cordially,*
> *Phoebe McPherson Montrose*

Fraser called to see if Niki had received the invitation and if she had put in for a leave of absence.

"Mum is really looking forward to meeting you."

"I hope you haven't built me up too much. I don't want her to be disappointed," Niki replied dubiously.

"Me? Exaggerate? No way," Fraser said, laughing.

Despite his assurances, Niki felt somewhat apprehensive about meeting Phoebe. Niki had created a picture in her mind of a rather austere Scotswoman, proud, independent, and capable. Left a widow with two small children at an early age, Phoebe had taken over from her uncle the management of a busy resort hotel and by all accounts had run it efficiently and profitably.

Fortunately, both Niki and Fraser were able to obtain leave that coincided. Fraser came up to London, and together they took the train to the Scottish highlands. From the small station they walked up the hilly cobblestone street to the McPherson Arms Hotel.

Phoebe greeted Niki warmly. Standing beside her tall son, Niki saw that they were very alike, at least in coloring. Phoebe's dark auburn hair was generously sprinkled with silver, but she had a smile that made her appear charmingly youthful. Simply dressed in a tweed skirt and cabled wool cardigan, she looked almost too young to be Fraser's mother. Her welcome was matched by that of his younger sister, Fiona, who was a graceful, slender girl with a blaze of beautiful flame-colored hair.

That evening there was a supper and dance, a small clan gathering held at the hotel, at which Niki had a chance to meet what seemed to her like dozens of Fraser's cousins. Every male had worn Highland dress, and Niki saw Fraser for the first time in kilt and tartan. He wore the vivid blue, green, and yellow Montrose-Graham plaid, while Phoebe's long skirt, worn with a black velvet jacket, displayed the McPherson colors. Fiona was the belle of the ball, Niki observed, claimed for every dance. The music was loud, lively, and the skirl of bagpipes was often heard. Niki was encouraged to take part in some of the traditional dances and was surprised to see that Fraser could do all of them with ease.

On Sunday they all attended church at the tiny, gray stone kirk where, Phoebe confided, she had been married to Jonathan Montrose. When they came outside after the service, a light mist was falling. It gave everything a blurred, unreal look. While Phoebe lingered to talk to the pastor and other friends, Fiona was surrounded by a group of young men.

"Come, I want to show you something," Fraser said, taking Niki's arm. He led her over to the entrance to the graveyard that adjoined the church property. They walked among the granite tombstones, reading the spare yet somehow poignant epitaphs. Many of the markers bore the name McPherson.

"I always assumed I'd be buried here with all my ancestors," Fraser remarked. "Now that's probably not true."

Niki glanced at him sharply. The remark was so unlike Fraser, it shocked her. He was normally so nonchalant, so carefree. She put a quick hand out, touched his arm. Immediately the serious look faded and a smile replaced it.

"Well, I didn't bring you out here to be gloomy. I had a sneakier reason. I wanted to give you this." He reached inside his tunic pocket, brought out a small box, and handed it to her.

Niki held the little box in both hands, looking up at Fraser.

"Go on, open it."

She pressed the spring and the lid popped open. Lying against purple velvet was a silver brooch, heart-shaped under an arching crown, with a small amethyst stone glistening in the center.

"Oh, Fraser, it's lovely."

"It seemed appropriate to give it to you here in the churchyard, in the shadow of the kirk. It's called a *luckenbooth,* and it's a traditional Scottish betrothal symbol. In the olden days couples went to church and in a special ceremony exchanged promises of their intention to be married. 'Plighting their troth,' it was called. . . ." He paused. "A betrothal was considered as binding as a marriage vow." He took the brooch out of her hands, held it for a minute, then asked, "Do you want me to pin it on?"

Niki nodded, speechless. Her own hands were too shaky to do it. Fraser fastened it on the lapel of her raincoat.

"So then, are we betrothed?" he asked. Putting one hand under her chin, he lifted it so he could search her eyes for his answer.

"Yes," she said in a very low voice. As Fraser took her into his arms, held her tightly against him, Niki closed her eyes, and a tear ran down her cheek. For the first time in her life she felt truly loved, truly safe, that she truly belonged.

Phoebe saw them off on the London train, loaded down with goodies from the hotel kitchen—packages of Scotch shortbread, jars of marmalade, lemon curd, butterscotch toffee. There was another box wrapped as a gift for Niki. "To be opened on the train," Phoebe told her as she said good-bye and kissed her on both cheeks. "God bless you both!"

As the train rolled across the bridge that led out of town, Niki unwrapped her gift. It was a tartan scarf in the Montrose plaid. Tears sprang into her eyes as she fingered the fine woolen cloth. She looked at Fraser.

"Does she know about me?" she asked. "I mean, that I'm not really a Montrose, that I'm an orphan?"

Fraser put his strong arm around her shoulders, pulled her close. "You're no orphan, Niki. You've got a new family now. You belong to us, and I'll never let you feel lost again. That I promise."

Back at Blanding Court, Alair tried to pick up her life again as it had been before Luc. But it was impossible. Something profound and life changing had happened to her.

She could hardly remember what it had been like before Luc or imagine what it would be like without him. Gradually those four days at Larkspur Cottage began to seem like a dream.

Unknown to—or only suspected by—most people, the Allies were gearing up to attack the Germans at their weakest, most vulnerable point, the Italian peninsula, Sicily. Luc's briefings changed drastically and his time off was shortened. For a month Luc and Alair shared only brief, abbreviated times together.

She threw herself into her work with the evacuee children again, many of whom had become special to her. She also now felt she had something more in common with their mothers. In spite of their different backgrounds, she felt the strong connection that her husband was united with theirs in an effort to defeat the enemy. To know they shared the constant anxiety that their men were in daily danger made Alair conscious of what the other women were feeling.

Soon Alair became aware of an even deeper bond. When she witnessed the brief, emotional reunions of these mothers with their children and then saw the wrenching good-byes, she could more easily imagine what it might be like to have to send your child away from you. Although she wasn't yet quite certain, Alair had the hope that she would soon be able to tell Luc they were going to have a child. She wanted to be quite sure before she told him.

Blanding Court had been in her father's family for generations, and like many of these ancient, sixteenth-century mansions, it contained a private chapel. Largely unused, it was pointed out to visitors as a relic of an earlier time. Alair now found it a refuge. Day after day she was drawn there. Kneeling on the ornately carved wooden kneeler with its tapestried pillow, she stared at the stained-glass windows over the small altar. Unlike the windows in great cathedrals, which depicted the saints, these portrayed illustrious Blanding ancestors attired in suits of armor or court robes. Alair prayed wordlessly, thinking that other women of this family before her might also have knelt here and prayed for husbands at war. How tragic that this had to be, that it was repeated generation after generation.

Alair wondered how she could survive this and had to determinedly place her trust in God. Surely he would protect Luc, bring him safely home to her.

At the thought of the child she was now assured would be born sometime in December, Alair's prayers became even more fervent. *God, let the end of this war truly bring the peace we are all praying for. Whether this baby is a boy or a girl, let it be possible that he or she will grow up in a safe world, the kind of world Luc believes in, is willing to fight for. . . .*

1944

chapter
23

Mayfield, Virginia
Cameron Hall
March 1944

THE PHONE RANG, piercing the quiet afternoon.

"I'll get it," Kitty offered, rising. "It's probably Craig. He said he'd call from Los Angeles." She went out to the hall, leaving Jill and Scott discussing the evening's plans.

Their conversation stopped abruptly when Kitty reentered the room with a face drained of color. She moved over to the table and, steadying herself on the back of one of the Heppewhite chairs, said in a voice that shook, "Something's happened. It's Luc."

A shocked silence followed. Then Scott asked, "What is it?"

Through stiff lips Jill asked, "Is he dead?"

"No, he was shot down, taken prisoner. That's all I know so far."

"One of us should go over to Montclair," Scott said, getting to his feet.

"I'll go," Kitty said quietly.

"Yes, maybe that would be best," Scott agreed.

"Give Cara and Kip our love, our sympathy," said Jill, knowing it would not be enough, wouldn't help.

"Of course." Kitty slipped on her jacket, picked up her handbag and car keys. "I'll let you know . . . later," she said as she went out of the room, out the front door.

Driving the short distance over to Montclair, Kitty's mind was in turmoil. What to say? In one way, under the devastating grief there was anger. Why, why? Kip had encouraged Luc, made him feel that joining the air force was the best way to serve. He had been inordinately proud of his son. It was almost as if Luc were his alter ego, his youth relived, as if Luc were experiencing the whole reckless adventure his father had pioneered.

When she walked into the house, she heard the raw sound of a man sobbing. Cara turned and looked at Kitty as she came into the living room. Her eyes were anguished. She stood beside Kip, whose head was down on his crossed arms on the table, his shoulders shaking.

Part of Kitty did not want to feel pity for him. She stood there, almost dispassionately watching, wanting to scream, *You wanted him to go. This is what happens when young men go to war!*—but that would be too cruel, inhuman. Kip needed more. He needed compassion. The words of a poem she loved came back into her mind: *"Loose me from tears and make me see how each hath back what once he stayed to weep: Homer his sight, David his little lad."*

Surely, God willing, Kip would have Luc back once this horrible war was over. At least Luc hadn't been killed. Whatever a German prison camp was like, there was still a chance that Kip and Luc would be reunited.

Montclair

It was gray dark when Cara woke up, the furniture hardly discernible in the dimness of the room. Kip's place beside her in the bed was empty. When had he got up, where had he gone? Probably to the air field. . . .

A glance at the bedside clock told her she had slept a good six hours. Still, she felt she had spent a sleepless night. The heaviness of yesterday's news hung like a weight over her as she dressed, went downstairs.

In the kitchen she made coffee. How did one go on doing the ordinary things of life when everything had changed, dreams had been shattered, the future diminished?

She got out cream, put the sugar bowl on the table, and answered her own question out loud. "But life is full of tragedy. You only need to pick up the paper; every day another disaster, somebody's tragedy."

Why was it people seemed to be able to withstand the big tragedies, with whatever inner source most people find? . . . It was the unexpected disasters that wounded the spirit, sickened the heart . . .

Kip, who had been called from the reserves to active duty, requested compassionate leave from his commanding officer and was granted it. As they waited for more news—where the prison camp was located, whether the Red Cross had been able to contact Luc, confirm the information—Kip remained devastated. Nothing seemed to help, not Cara's support or others' sympathy.

Although Kitty's heart ached for him, Cara knew that underneath, her twin dealt with her resentment of the past, saying Kip had encouraged Luc to learn to fly, almost as if he had wanted to replay his own youth. What would Kitty have had Luc do? Be a conscientious objector like Gareth?

But Gareth's feelings were deep-rooted, bred into him by his father from boyhood. If anyone had a reason to want to go fight, defeat the enemy, especially the Japanese, it was Gareth. His beloved was a prisoner trapped in who knew what horrible conditions, from whom he hadn't heard for two years.

No, to be fair, it had been Luc's own choice to become a pilot, join the air force. Maybe he had unconsciously needed to prove something to his father, if nothing else. Would Kip ever have his son back? Well, if he could survive a German POW camp, he might still come home.

Kip had to report back to duty before they received definite confirmation of the name and location of Luc's prison camp.

England

When Niki heard about Luc being shot down and taken prisoner, she was devastated. She thought of Tante and Uncle Kip, what they must be going through. And Aunt Kitty, who had loved Luc and hated the war. When Bryanne called her from Birchfields to tell her, Niki had for the rest of the day moved around as in a walking nightmare. She lived the scene in her mind—the shrapnel-riddled plane, the ball of fire, the spiraling downward plunge, the explosion on the ground. Evidently Luc had parachuted out but was injured, couldn't escape, and was captured. All Alair had received was an official notice that he was now a prisoner of war.

Niki thought of their wedding day. No two people had ever seemed more in love. Alair had been a picture, and Luc had gazed at her with such devotion. . . . Niki's heart wrenched as she remembered. She should write to Alair. But what could she say? Were there any words that could help? Alair was in that lonely place where sometime everyone who loves has to walk.

Fear gripped Niki. It had happened to Luc. Luc, who had always seemed invincible to her. As far back as she could remember, Luc had been in her life. More than a brother, a friend, the one person in her world that she knew had loved her unconditionally all these years. He had stood up for her, stood by her; even when he wasn't convinced she knew what she was doing, he had fought for her. She had never believed anything bad could happen to Luc.

If it could happen to Luc, no one she loved was safe. Niki clenched her hands, brought them to her mouth, bit down on her knuckles to stem the agonized sobs that rushed from deep inside. Fraser. She knew he was in dangerous work. He couldn't talk about it; it was top secret. But he had been training with his unit down at the coast, cliff climbing. The rumors were that those units were preparing for the coming invasion of France. She shivered with dread.

Niki touched the small luckenbooth brooch she wore pinned to the lining of her uniform jacket. Betrothed. She and Fraser were promised to each other as surely, as solemnly, as if they had already taken marriage vows.

If anything happened to Fraser, she couldn't stand it.

The irony of the tragedy came only a month later. Before they had verifiable information about Luc, Kip was killed. In a routine flight delivering a B-52 bomber from an air base in Texas to another in North Carolina, his plane disappeared, mysteriously went down somewhere in the mountains of Tennessee.

chapter
24

THE DAY OF KIP'S memorial service, the Mayfield church was packed. People who had known Kip since childhood, had been friends and neighbors of both the Montrose and Cameron families, were represented there. A group of others who had come out of respect and love but could not be seated in the small sanctuary was clustered outside on the steps and in the courtyard.

Kitty sat beside Cara in the Montrose family pew, feeling her sister's pain as if it were her own. At one time it could have been she who was newly widowed, grieving for the man who never quite grew up, the boy they had both loved. Perhaps he had died in a way he might have chosen.

Cara had been composed but numbed, so Kitty had made the funeral arrangements. With Cara's approval, she found something appropriate to be read at the close of the service. It was a poem written by a young British airman. Kitty felt even Kip, who professed to be "illiterate," would have loved it.

Oh, I have slipped the surly bonds of earth
And danced the skies on laughter's silvered wings:
Sunward I've climbed and joined the tumbling mirth
Of sun-split clouds, and done a hundred things
You have not dreamed of, wheeled and soared and swung

High in the sunlit silence, hovering there,
I've chased the shouting wind along and flung
My eager craft through footless halls of air.
Up, up the long delirious, burning blue
I've topped the windswept heights with easy grace
Where never lark, or even eagle, flew.
And while, with silent lifting mind I've trod
The high untrespassed sanctity of space,
Put out my hand, and touched the face of God.*

The young minister, soon to leave to become an army chaplain himself, read the poem with great emotion. The hush that followed showed how moved by it everyone was.

Cara turned to Kitty, her eyes bright with tears, and whispered, "We must send a copy of this to Luc."

They regularly sent Red Cross packages to Luc in the German prison camp, not knowing whether he got them or would get the sad news of his father's death. How strange that Kip had suffered the loss of his son and now it was the son who had lost his father.

Kitty remembered the poem she had recalled at the time they received the news of Luc's being shot down, taken prisoner. She had prayed then that Kip would someday "have back what once he stayed to weep"—his son. Now she knew it would not be in this life, but she had the assurance that one day, however far off, father and son would be reunited.

At the graveside Cara accepted the folded flag that had draped Kip's coffin. Kitty prayed she would not have to accept another one later for Luc. She remembered the horror stories told by Allied prisoners after World War I. In 1918 Germany was considered a Christian country, not the godless nation it was now.

---

*Author John Gillespie Magee. Reproduced by permission from *This England* magazine.

Back at Montclair, after all the family and friends had left, Cara sat alone at the kitchen table, sipping tea. She was alone as she had not been in years. Niki was in England, Luc who knew where? And Kip—she kept listening for his footstep, his call, knowing it would never come again.

When Niki read the account of Kip's funeral printed in the *Mayfield Messenger* sent to her by Cara, she wept as she had not wept since the news of Luc's capture. Kip dead was something she could hardly imagine. He had always been larger than life to her. The tall, strong American who had appeared at the orphanage when she was four years old had remained in her heart and mind as her idol. He had been more than a father; he had been the enduring symbol of security and unconditional love. She could not remember a time when he had scolded or corrected. Kip had always left the discipline to Cara. He had laughed a lot, hugged a lot, loved her just as he had loved Luc, his own son. Now Kip was gone from her life forever, and she would never be able to fill the void he left.

Kip's memory echoed through the silent house. The emptiness of the large home reflected the great emptiness within Cara. With Kip, a part of herself was gone forever. Whatever had happened between them in their childhood, their lives, their marriage, her life had been inexorably bound up in his. There had been too many years, too many shared experiences; there were too many bonds tying them together, even into eternity.

In the weeks that followed Kip's funeral, more and more Cara realized it was impossible for her to manage the stable and the acreage by herself. She sold all but three of the horses—hers, Luc's, and Niki's. Someday Luc and Niki would both come home. In the meantime the Pony Club lessons were suspended. People were busy with war work. Even the children were busily occupied in various collection efforts—aluminum cans, foil, rubber bands.

The house was achingly lonely for one person. Montclair was meant to be full of the sounds of life, of children's voices, of doors opening and slamming, of laughter, music, and running feet on the stairway. It had ceased to be a home, had become an empty shell.

Cara spent many sleepless nights walking the floor, going in and out of the rooms, trying to decide what to do. Finally she determined she couldn't continue living here alone. She looked into the possiblility of renting Montclair for the duration. However, realtors reminded her that since it was wartime, there'd be no interest unless she wanted to turn it over to the government for some purpose such as to provide a rest and rehabilitation center for servicemen. These days, with all the shortages of civilian help and workers needed to maintain such a large estate, it would be too much responsibility for an individual. Montclair had once required twenty servants to keep its high-ceilinged rooms dusted, the furniture polished, the floors shiny, the windows sparkling. And the grounds—well, where could you get gardeners nowadays? Discouraged, Cara came to the conclusion that the best thing to do was to close it for the present. God willing, after the war Luc would be coming home, taking over the magnificent heritage of his father, grandfather, and ancestors. Until then the house would be waiting for him.

Cara was unsure what she would do next, but she knew that eventually she would be guided as to what her purpose should be. How could she contribute to the country's war effort? There must be something she could do. She went to the local Red Cross board, applied for any sort of work for which her previous war experience might qualify her. Much to her surprise, within two weeks she was assigned to the army hospital near Richmond as a program facilitator.

It was with a sense of anticipation mixed with nostalgia that she prepared to leave Montclair for her new job. There was a finality about it. Cara was too much an optimist to imagine she was leaving forever. She held on to the hope that some happier day she would come back, that one day Luc and his children would live here. She closed the door for the last time and placed the key under the mat as she had always done.

chapter

25

Blanding Court

WHEN ALAIR HAD RECEIVED the tersely worded official notification of Luc's capture, it had given his name, rank, and prison number. She had read it over and over until at last she had absorbed the terrible truth. She kept that paper folded and with her all the time; it somehow made her feel connected with Luc.

But try as she might, she couldn't imagine where he was, what his day was like as hers inched agonizingly by. She had been told that certain international rules governed the imprisonment of officers. Not that that meant anything now to the Nazis. Stories of the atrocities perpetrated by occupying troops in all the countries they had subjugated—Holland, Belgium, France—had been fed to the British public in every newspaper. She had no assurance that enemy prisoners, be they officers or not, would receive any kind of civilized treatment.

When the letters began to trickle in from him, few and far between as they were, censored and brief, she clung to them as if to a lifeline. She read them until their edges were ragged. He said little about his daily life.

Thinking of you, I find I can't remember anything the world thinks important, just the times spent with you. I treasure each tiny memory. You are kept safe, locked forever in my heart. Hold on to this promise, for I intend to keep it—we will get through this and be together again.

Ever yours,
Luc

Alair held on to these words, believing that with God's help, Luc's promise would come true for them.

Niki had been transferred and reassigned and was now translating communiqués from the French underground to various Allied services. This fact somewhat made up for her crushing disappointment of not going with her team into occupied France. Niki felt that what she was doing now was more worthwhile than her former work as a teleprinter operator. It also kept her from the enervating depression that threatened to overwhelm her when she thought about Kip and Luc. One afternoon as she came off duty, she was told, "Gilbreaux, you have a visitor."

Niki hurried down to the lounge, thinking it might be Fraser. Perhaps he'd received an unexpected leave. But when she got to the entryway, she saw a man in the uniform of the Free French standing with his back to the door, looking out the window. By the set of his shoulders, the shape of his head, she recognized him. It was Paul. At the sound of her footsteps he turned, and for a few seconds they simply stared at each other.

Finally she gasped his name. "Paul!"

He came toward her. He looked older. His face was lean, his cheekbones prominent, his features sharpened, his eyes wary. He held out his hands and she placed hers in them. Then he leaned forward, kissed her on both cheeks in the French manner.

"Niki, *Cherie*," he said. "Have you forgiven me?"

"Oh, Paul, yes, long ago," she responded spontaneously,

momentarily wondering what might have happened if he hadn't cut her from the mission. That was all past now, in light of everything else that had happened. "You've heard about Luc?" she asked. From the pained expression that crossed his face, she knew that he had.

"Yes. I've lost many comrades, but Luc was more like a brother. It's hard to shrug and say *c'est la guerre* when it comes to someone you love. But Luc will survive. If anyone can, he will. He's strong."

"And he has something to come home to now. His wife is expecting their baby."

"Ah, *c'est bon*. I think we're beginning to see some light, a possibility of victory in all this darkness." He paused, then asked, "Your new assignment. You like it?"

"I'm good at it. It helps to know you're doing something that may help end this awful war."

"What you're doing here is good, Niki. Not everyone could do it. It may not seem exciting or daring, but it is important. Believe me." Paul shifted his coat sleeve and looked at his watch. "I must go, *Cherie*."

"Oh, Paul, can't you stay? We could go somewhere . . ."

He shook his head. "I have meetings, and—" He halted. "I came here mainly to see you. I felt bad about how we parted. I was afraid I'd made you feel somehow—"

"That I didn't measure up? Well, yes, for a while I did." She smiled. "But then someone I care about very much suggested that it might not have been God's plan for my life. That made me feel better about it."

Paul lifted his eyebrows. "Someone you care about very much?" he repeated. "Are you in love, Niki?"

"I think so. Yes." She smiled again. "I wish you knew him. You'd like him. He's like Luc in some ways. Actually, they're cousins. Maybe someday we'll all meet."

"Someday. Let us devoutly pray so, *Cherie*," Paul sighed. "No matter what happens, I shall always remember that last day in Paris. You, Luc, and I, we took a picnic, sat on the bank of the Seine. We were so young, so happy. Do you remember?"

"Of course I remember," Niki said, feeling the tears gather in her eyes.

"Now I really must go," Paul said.

She walked out to the hall with him. At the door they embraced. *"Au revoir, Cherie,"* Paul whispered. "The French farewell is so much more optimistic than the English. And we shall see each other again."

Don't know where, don't know when. The words of the song she and Fraser called their own echoed in Niki's mind. They kissed and Paul left. As she watched Paul go down the steps, Niki hated the war more intensely than she ever had.

chapter
26

TWO WEEKS LATER Niki found a note in her mailbox that read, "Urgent, call number"—it was a number she recognized. Fraser's quarters. It took ages to get through to him. The circuits were busy. The connection, never good in this time of war, was terrible. There were beeps, squeaks, and buzzes on the line. When Fraser finally answered, his voice was tense. Immediately Niki's alarm flags went up. He told her in guarded terms that his training was completed and he had a weekend pass. From the tone of his voice Niki felt a shiver of fear. There was more to this message. Her hand clutched the receiver compulsively. She was experienced enough now in the way of war to know that what Fraser wasn't able to tell her was that he was being sent overseas.

"Can you get some time, meet me somewhere?" he asked. She heard the urgency in his voice. "I have three days."

"I'll try," she said breathlessly, already frantically grasping for a reason to ask for leave. Family emergency? Did her tenuous connection to Fraser qualify as a *family* relationship? Would her commanding officer be more lenient, be more likely to grant her leave, if Niki frankly said it was her fiancé who was leaving for unknown battle duty?

As it turned out, in checking her file it was found that she had accumulated time off, and her papers were signed forthwith.

Hardly able to believe her luck, Niki phoned Fraser back. The line was faulty; squeaks and crackling noises made it hard to hear. "Got a pencil?" Fraser asked "Write this down. I'll meet you there. I've made all the arrangements." They rang off. Niki folded the piece of paper on which she had jotted down the information Fraser had dictated and stuffed it into her jacket pocket. Then she ran upstairs to pack.

Elly came off duty while Niki was packing. "Where are you off to?"

"Got three days," Niki replied and went on packing, folding things with elaborate care.

"You sure you're not off to some romantic rendezvous?" Elly teased. Niki's hands froze. Had Elly hit the mark? All the unspoken thoughts, questions, that had raced through her own mind during Fraser's call now surfaced. What had Fraser in mind? If he was going off into the thick of things and this was the last time they'd be together, did he . . . ?

"You are such a nut!" Niki retorted as casually as she could manage. Then she turned with a swift movement and bent over her bag again, as if checking the contents before closing it.

Elly didn't say anything more, just gathered up her toilet bag and wandered down to the showers. Niki wondered how much her roommate suspected. But there wasn't time to figure that out or try to explain. She had to get to the train station, hope she could get on the first train to the town where Fraser was supposed to meet her, a short distance outside London.

London looked old, gray, dirty. It was a city at war, battered, streets lined with bombed-out and boarded-up buildings. Most of the people were in uniform. Sandbags were piled on sidewalks. Arrowed signs pointed to air-raid shelters.

The huge train station was crowded as usual, thronged with service men and women. Clutching her ticket, Niki pushed through and was propelled along with others down the platform and finally onto a train car.

For the first time in the last frantic hours, Niki had a chance to think of what she was doing, where this was leading. She dug out the scrap of paper and studied it. Windsong Inn. Niki took a long, trembling breath. How romantic that sounded.

At the small train station she was given directions.

"'Tis a pleasant walk, Miss," the weary-looking station manager told her kindly, tipping his hat.

When the Windsong Inn came into sight, Niki saw it was the English inn of all the tourist brochures. A rambling Tudor building painted white with crossed timbers and a sloping roof. A garden in front and a brick pathway leading to an arched blue door under a trellis trailing with roses. Too quaint? Or just right?

So this is where Fraser had arranged to meet. Niki's heart beat painfully hard. At the gate leading into the garden she hesitated. Fraser had once mentioned that his friend, Plover, had offered them the use of an aunt's cottage for a weekend. Niki had never responded to his implied possibility. She had realized that she had only to say the word and it could be theirs.

They were in love, there was no question of that. If it were not for the war, they would no doubt be making wedding plans. That was in some hazy future. A future that was, hour by hour, moving out of their reach. There was no more time for planning or patience.

Being together for however long was all that mattered. To live in the present was all the choice they had. With the world splintering around them, why should they not be together?

Niki pushed open the gate, walked along the garden path and into the house. Inside, the pink-cheeked, gray-haired woman behind the registration desk greeted Niki warmly. "Oh yes, Lieutenant Montrose made reservations. I'm Mrs. Dahglen, the hostess. Dinner is served at eight. You'll have time to rest and change if you like. He phoned to say he might be delayed, but he said to assure you he'd be here as soon as possible."

The room to which Niki was shown was bright with flowered chintz, but under the ruffled curtains at the dormer windows were blackout blinds. Instructions posted on the door said, "Pull blinds securely after dark."

Even that reminder that it was wartime seemed unreal in this charming place, Niki thought. Moving as one in a dream, she took off her uniform and changed into the dress she had worn the night she and Fraser had met for the second time at Birchfields. It was one that Fraser particularly liked. It was prewar, velvet, the shade of a ripe plum. It was simply styled with a jewel neckline, long sleeves. Lastly she pinned the luckenbooth brooch to the bodice.

Too restless to remain in her room, Niki went downstairs. She peeked into the dining room, where a few early diners were seated. The room was dark; flickering candles on each table gave it an intimate atmosphere. The tables were placed all around the room, at discreet distances from each other so conversations could not be overheard. A fireplace set into an old-fashioned inglenook burned cheerily.

Niki's heart gave an excited little lift. Soon Fraser would be here. They would sit, hands touching across the table, eyes feasting on each other. She sighed in anxious anticipation. Until he came, she decided she would take a walk in the garden that beckoned invitingly.

She went outside and was enchanted by what she found. Some romantic had fashioned a dream here, created for lovers to stroll through in leisurely enjoyment. A waterfall divided the garden, flowing down over rocks and flowers, its spray plinking softly into the pool as it descended. The trees bending over either side added to the mysterious magic of the place.

Quite suddenly Niki felt melancholy. It was sad to be alone in this fairy-tale setting—like being alone at the Taj Mahal in moonlight. What was needed was a hand to hold, enriching the moment with the sweetness of familiarity. It would be doubly romantic to be with someone you adored, someone who was devoted to you.

"Fraser, my love. Hurry!" she whispered.

Just then she heard footsteps on the gravel path behind and turned in happy expectation. But it wasn't Fraser. It was Mrs. Dahglen.

"There's a phone call for you. If you'll come, you can take it in my parlor in private," the innkeeper told her.

Niki followed her inside and into the cozy little parlor behind the registration desk.

She picked up the receiver, said a breathless hello, and heard that familiar voice with its identifying burr. "Darling, it's Fraser. Orders changed. I . . . I can't meet you. I'm so terribly sorry. In a matter of hours. That's all I can tell you, except I love you and I would give all I have if things were different." His voice was tight with stress, disappointment.

Niki felt weak. No, this couldn't be happening! All she managed to say was, "Then you're not coming?"

"I can't." His answer was brisk, almost curt. Then in a rush of words he said, "Niki, I love you more than I can ever tell you. I tried to get a special license, permission from my commanding officer, so we could be married this weekend. . . . I wanted it all to be so perfect. Oh, darling—" His voice broke.

Her hand gripped the phone. "I know. I understand. It can't be helped." She wanted to tell him that permission or not, license or not, she loved him now and forever. There was so much she wanted to say. But now there wasn't time for anything but good-bye.

Although she didn't think she would, being worn out with tears and weariness, Niki slept deeply. She awoke to the patter of rain on the crisscross panes of the bedroom windows. She stretched her arms, feeling the smoothness of the linen sheets, which smelled lightly of lavender, and snuggled into the down comforter as she came slowly awake.

Then gradually awareness returned. Fraser was on a troop train going somewhere. To France? Would she ever see him again? A sob caught in her throat as she remembered yesterday and what this morning might have been.

She got up and put her uniform back on and went downstairs. Breakfast was being served in the dining room. The morning meal cheered her a little, gave her strength. She hadn't eaten dinner but had gone straight to her room after the phone call from Fraser. She hadn't had such food in months. Fresh apple muffins, country butter, amber honey shimmering in a glass container.

Afterward when she stopped to settle the bill, Mrs. Dahglen said, "Oh, the lieutenant took care of everything beforehand." Her blue eyes were sympathetic. "It's too bad it didn't work out, dear. But then, maybe it's all for the best. Who knows? The Lord does, we can count on that."

On the walk back to the small station to catch her train back to London, Niki thought about what the woman had said. Yes, she was probably right. Maybe the Lord did know best. She had to believe that. If this weekend was not theirs, then God had something better for them. Niki felt confirmation flow through her. It was almost as if God were promising that he would take care of Fraser, protect him, bring him back, so that they could really be together—forever, in God's timing.

Birchfields
December 1944

The persistent ring startled Garnet out of a sound sleep. Her heart pounding, she sat up in bed, reached for the phone in the dark. Her fumbling hand knocked it off its hook, and before she could grab it she had to first turn on the lamp beside the bed. As she did, she looked at the clock. It was four in the morning. Christmas morning.

"Hello," she said breathlessly into the mouthpiece.

"Grandmother, it's Bryanne."

"Yes, darling, what is it?" Garnet clutched the phone.

"It's Alair, Grandmother. She's had her baby. It's a boy, a sweet, healthy baby."

"Oh, my dear, I'm so glad, so relieved. And Alair?"

"She's fine. Tired but so happy. She sends her love."

"And give her mine. I'll tell the others." Garnet's voice shook a little.

She put down the receiver and took a deep breath.

Pushing the pillows behind her back, she sat up in bed. A new baby. A little boy. Born on Christmas Day. What a special blessing. What a special little baby. It was a sign of hope, of life renewed. How pleased his father would be when he knew. She wondered how long it would take to give Luc the happy news. They'd have to go through the Red Cross to get word to him in a German prison camp to tell him of his son's birth. Dear God, have mercy. On all the men whose sons are born in this awful time. Let this birth be some kind of symbol that the world will never let a war like this happen again.

That's what we said the last time, Garnet reflected. *This is what Kitty tried to say in her book. But we did let it happen again.*

Well, she was not going to be morbid. Not today. Today was a celebration of Christ's birth, and Luc's son shared it. They were having a wonderful party today for all the men under this roof, men who were recuperating, putting their bodies, minds, and emotions back together. Today she would do everything she could possibly do to make this a glorious, happy day for everyone.

1945

chapter
27

Birchfields
May 1945

GARNET WATCHED FROM THE TERRACE as the last car disappeared around the curve of the driveway. She had sent them all away to the celebration taking place in the town hall and everywhere in the village. The long-prayed-for peace had finally come with the announcement of Germany's surrender. Church bells had rung, and there had been shouts, cheers, hugs and tears, dancing and singing. All day long "There'll Always Be an England" and "Hail Britannia" were being sung in schoolrooms and pubs and being played over the radio. Occasionally, even such songs as "Yankee Doodle" and "Over There" were also heard. *And for good reason*, Garnet thought. After all, the Americans had helped bring about this glorious day. The brilliant strategist General Eisenhower, working with Britain's flamboyant General "Monty" Montgomery, hero of the North African campaign against Rommel, had accomplished the successful invasion of Normandy. Of course, it was the retaliatory bombing of Germany that had brought about the German surrender. Garnet shuddered. War!

Thank God it was over. It had been a long five years, and at times the future had looked very bleak indeed. Providentially, this part of England had been spared much of the devastation that other places, less remote and more important, had suffered. Still, everyone was exhausted. For all the excited elation she had felt earlier when the news of victory was officially announced over the BBC, Garnet felt a little weak and shaky now. She hadn't realized what a toll these past years had taken. "Feeling my age, I guess," she murmured out loud, something she might not have admitted if anyone else had been around to hear. However, she was alone. Bryanne had been reluctant to leave her, but Garnet had insisted. Steven had driven over from the hospital to share the news, and Garnet had urged them to go with the others to the village celebration. They had both earned it. Steven had worked tirelessly as a medical officer, and Bryanne had not only managed the hospitality weekends at Birchfields but also headed the local Red Cross. They had a right to be part of the joyful celebration.

Today had been wonderful, but now Garnet was feeling tired. She would go to her bedroom and relax. Before going inside, she paused to look over her garden. It needed work. At the beginning of the war, they had turned some of the flower beds into planting areas for vegetables. Now she could plan to bring it back to its former magnificence. Men would be returning; she could get gardeners again. She would have to decide which bulbs she wanted. Tulips perhaps, all colors, if poor Holland's fields had not been completely ruined during the Nazi occupation. Garnet sighed, leaned heavily on her cane. So much to do. She went inside. The house was strangely quiet, because Garnet had let her small household staff go off as well.

Upstairs Garnet stretched out on her chaise lounge. Things had been so hectic, she hadn't even taken time to read the newspaper. She put on her reading specs, unfolded the paper, and skimmed the bold headlines on the front page, then turned to Grace Comfort's column.

Several weeks before, when Lenora and Victor Ridgeway were visiting Birchfields, Victor had told Garnet that he had already written the column they would use when victory finally was declared. "By writing it, I was standing on my conviction that in the end good would overcome evil, right would prevail, that the human race is still capable of grand and noble deeds."

Privately, Garnet had always felt that Victor, writing as Grace Comfort, was a bit over the edge optimistically, sentimentally. Still, she was curious to read what he had written before VE Day.

Ten minutes later she laid the paper aside. For once Garnet had no criticism of the column. The last lines were particularly satisfactory. He had quoted the American president Abraham Lincoln, whom Garnet, as well as many other Southerners, had come belatedly to admire: "I am writing this in faith and with the strong hope that it will be true for us who have believed and fought so bravely for it. Peace will come soon and come to stay and so come as to be worth keeping in all future time."

Garnet was glad she had lived to see this day. Her heart echoed the expressed hope for a lasting peace so that Luc and Alair's little son would never know the horrors of war. She had lived through four wars. What a lot of memories she had. . . . She had been blessed with an incredibly long life . . . had known grief, hardship, sorrow, joys . . . mostly blessings. Yes, it had been a long, rich life. . . . She had known so much love. She thought of her parents, of Bryce Montrose, who had loved her, of Malcolm, whom she had loved and lost. He had broken her heart twice, once when he married the beautiful Rose Meredith, a second time when he had brought Blythe home from California. . . . Maybe it was all for the best. Who knows? If that had not happened, she might never have met Jeremy or had Faith. . . . God had generously blessed her. She had no regrets. Well, perhaps a few. She wished she had been kinder, more understanding, less stubborn . . . but God knows and forgives. . . .

Garnet leaned her head back against the satin pillows, closed her eyes. Dusk was gathering in the garden, and in the pale early evening sky the shadow outline of the moon could be seen over the tops of the trees. No need to fear the moonlight tonight, thank God. As the room darkened, Garnet thought vaguely that she should get up, turn on some lamps, but this was so pleasant, so peaceful, she would just lie here a little while longer and rest . . .

Garnet Cameron Devlin

The simple headstone was placed next to Jeremy's in the small cemetery of the village church where she had worshiped since coming to live in England.

When the will was read, Birchfields had been left to Bryanne. Garnet had expressed the suggestion that Steven might want to use it as a convalescent home for veterans. She left them free to decide its best purpose; her only wish was that they rename it for her beloved daughter Faith Devlin Montrose.

The name and the allocation seemed very appropriate to Bryanne and Steven, and they were happy to carry out her grandmother's request.

chapter
28

THE TRAIN PULLED TO A STOP with a hissing of brakes. Compartment doors banged open with a series of clatters, and uniformed men and women flowed off onto the platform. The station was thronged with people, all kinds, all shapes, all sizes. Old people, young, children wild with excitement, jumping up and down, women with eager faces, carrying bouquets of flowers, a sea of uniforms mingled with the mixture of civilians.

Fraser, towering over most, stepped out into the crowd. Where was Niki? Had she got his telegram? Or had it possibly been routed wrong? His gaze swept over the milling people, searching for the face he wanted most in the world to see. His eyes rested momentarily on a small, slight girl in a flowered hat who was frantically waving, but then went right past her. He was looking for the trim figure in the familiar blue WRENS uniform. He was looking for the face in the small photo he'd carried in his wallet all these months. Its wide, expressive eyes, sparkling with mischief one moment, pensive or troubled the next, eyes that had been brilliant with tears when he and Niki had said goodbye a few months ago. He thought of her small, pretty nose, the generous mouth he loved to kiss. Where in blazes was she?

He frowned fiercely. Was there some other reason she hadn't come to meet him? Had she met someone else? Changed her mind? His heart gave a lurch.

"Fraser! Fraser!" he heard his name called. "Over here!"

He turned in the direction of the voice he recognized. Suddenly everything stopped; all the noise around him receded. It was Niki's voice. He saw her then, through the mass of people pushing against him. He started toward her, feeling as if he were wading in quicksand. He kept her in focus. No wonder he hadn't spotted her at first. She was wearing a ridiculous little hat, and a ruffled collar framed her face. But she looked great—beautiful, in fact.

At last he reached her. She was standing absolutely still, but when he opened his arms, she flung herself into them. His arms went around her, lifting her off her feet. She was so light that he was almost afraid he might crush her.

Tears were running down her cheeks. He'd have to do something with that silly veil in order to wipe them away and kiss her. He set her down and she looked up at him. With both gloved hands she folded back the veil. At last Fraser kissed her, knocking the foolish little hat sideways, a kiss that settled for both of them all doubts that their love was real, that it had endured the long separation, and that they belonged to each other "from this day forward."

Mayfield, Virginia
September 1945

The sound of church bells ringing broke through the somnolent quiet of the September day. Almost spontaneously people began arriving at the Mayfield church. Others drifted in until the small sanctuary was filled and people were standing along the sides from the back to the altar rail. Hearts were full and eyes glistened as friends greeted one another, exchanging smiles, murmurs, and hugs, expressing their deep gratitude that finally the war that had lasted nearly four years, hovering over their daily lives, was over.

There was hardly a person or a family who had not been touched in some way by the war. As they gathered in thanksgiving for victory, they were not unmindful of those who were not here. The ones who would never come here again to worship, pray, and sing hymns, would never see their children grow up, marry, or bring a baby here to be christened.

They knew nothing would ever be quite the same. Not for anyone, neither the ones who were here nor the ones whose return they awaited nor the ones lost to them forever. However, although the moment was not undimmed by tears, everyone was aware that it was a moment that would always stay in their memories. God had brought them through a time of testing, and they were humbly grateful.

Reverend Morrison, whose two sons were still overseas, entered the church. The murmurs of the congregation faded away to a respectful hush as he proceeded up the middle aisle, went through the chancel gate, mounted the pulpit.

"Dear friends," he began, and his voice broke. Nearly overcome with emotion, he paused to compose himself before going on. "Rejoice, again I say, rejoice." His voice trembled but gradually grew stronger. "This is the day we have longed for, prayed for. This is the day the Lord has made; let us rejoice and be glad. Glory be to God." He bowed his head and brought out a large handkerchief from under his surplice and wiped his eyes, blew his nose. Then he signaled to Mrs. Creighton, who was already seated at the organ, and said, "Let us sing the hymn inspired from Isaiah 52:7." Without a moment's hesitation she played the opening chords to "Our God Reigns."

"How lovely on the mountains are the feet of him who brings good news, good news . . . ," voices sang out. "Announcing peace, proclaiming news of happiness, our God reigns, our God reigns."

Never had the song been sung as loud or as enthusiastically as it was that afternoon. Never had it been sung with such fervor or meaning. Each person's heart lifted as the triumphant words were repeated over and over.

Usually the service in this church was dignified, the ancient rituals conducted in quiet order. Today, however, the people seemed to forget the decorum that since childhood they had been taught to observe within these sacred walls. Yet never had a service seemed as appropriate. No one who attended that day would ever forget it. They would remember it as a fitting tribute to the God they worshiped, who had brought them through a terrible time and once more blessed America with peace.

At last the wonderful news came that the war was ended in the Pacific as well as in Europe. The Japanese had surrendered. Peace had come. Brooke would be freed, Gareth thought with a wary heart. *Please, God,* he prayed.

Through Aunt Cara at the Red Cross and the connection of Senator Frank Maynard, Gareth was able to get information about Japanese prisoners of war, the nonmilitary internees. He was at Avalon when the cable came and was rerouted to him.

American national Brooke Leslie was alive, being repatriated to the United States aboard a ship leaving Japan, via Hawaii, and would dock in San Diego. Gareth rejoiced, gave thanks, and immediately made preparations to go to California to meet Brooke's ship. They would be married and he would bring her home to Avalon.

chapter
29

San Diego, California

EVERY MUSCLE IN GARETH'S BODY TENSED, every nerve tingled, as he stood among the crowd waiting for the great ship to dock. All around him people looked up at the passengers leaning against the railing above, shouting and waving excitedly and receiving shouts and waves in return. The compressed excitement was tangible. As the gangplank was lowered, secured, the throng surged forward. Who knew how long everyone there had prayed, yearned, longed, for this moment when they would be reunited with loved ones, not even knowing if they were alive or dead?

Gareth's heart pounded heavily as the gate at the top of the gangplank was lifted back and passengers began to descend. He felt bodies pressing against him from behind. He moved involuntarily as people pushed forward. His eyes searched frantically the streams of passengers for the one face he had carried so long in his mind, in his heart's memory. His pulse thrummed and his breath was coming in short gasps.

Then he saw her. His stomach wrenched painfully. In shock, in relief. She was coming slowly down the ramp. There was another woman beside her. They were arm in arm. Who was supporting whom? Was Brooke holding on to the woman, or was it the other way around? They moved haltingly. Gareth's throat was dry and tight from anxiety. Was she ill? The pressure of the crowd behind him inched him toward the bottom of the gangplank. Soon he would be able to reach out and touch her. Now he saw her more clearly. Dear God, she was thin. Thinner than he ever remembered. But then, how could she not be, with all those months of deprivation? And her hair was threaded with silvery streaks waving back from her high forehead. What she must have endured. Gareth felt the horrors he'd imagined confirmed. But her eyes, now sweeping the crowd for him, were still lovely and violet blue in the pale oval of her face.

"Brooke!" he yelled. "Here I am!" He lifted one arm, waving wildly.

In another few minutes they were in each other's arms. He felt her fragility through the flimsy material of the dress she was wearing and loosened his hold. "Oh, dearest, dearest Gareth," he heard her husky whisper. "I was so afraid you might not have got my cable. There were so many being sent. I was terrified you wouldn't be here."

He could not answer for the enormous lump blocking all the words he wanted to say. Brooke was here, she was safe, the agony was over. That was enough for now.

His arm around her securely, he maneuvered her through the dense crowd, where other equally emotional, dramatic reunions were taking place. "My grandmother lent me her car," he told her. "Where are your things?"

She held up the small valise she was carrying. "This is all. The few things the Red Cross supplied for us, hardly more than a toothbrush, some underclothes. I don't mean to sound ungrateful. What few supplies I nursed in the camps make this a luxury." Brooke managed a laugh that sounded delightful to Gareth.

"We'll get you whatever you need or want," he promised.

They drove down the coast to the Riverside Inn. Gareth was never sure exactly how he managed the highway traffic to get there. He was so conscious of Brooke beside him, he might easily have been too distracted to drive safely. Somehow within hours they were there.

Lunching on the patio, they could hardly eat for gazing into each other's eyes, breaking off in the middle of a sentence about something else to say wonderingly, "I can't believe you're really here" and "I prayed for this moment and now that it's here, it seems unreal."

They went to the little shopping center of Spanish-style architecture, its arched, vine-covered walkways between stores of every kind. There Brooke made a few purchases. Afterward they wandered hand in hand, stopping to browse and window-shop, still too aware of each other to be really present where they were.

On the way back to the hotel, they passed the ancient mission, now a tourist attraction rather than a place of worship. It seemed natural to slow to a stop. Gareth pulled into a parking space in front of the building. He turned to Brooke questioningly. She said quietly, "We have so much to be thankful for."

Gareth nodded. "So many answered prayers."

It seemed entirely appropriate that they go inside, even though it was not the parish church it had been long ago. They entered the dim old chapel with its adobe walls, tiled floor, worn benches, and knelt down, lifting grateful hearts to the God who had been so faithful.

"May the Lord watch between me and thee when we are absent from each other. Genesis 31:49," whispered Brooke, slipping her hand into Gareth's. "I said that over and over every day." She remembered the small Bible she had carried into the Japanese internment camp with her, the one she still had.

They remained for a few more minutes in the quiet, then left, still caught up in the solemnity of the moment.

That evening they had dinner served on the balcony outside their room, which looked out onto the mountain, where a sunset began spreading its palette of glorious colors across the sky. They talked of many things, of that summer so long ago when they had fallen in love, of the things that had happened in the years since, and then of the future.

"I can't wait to take you home, Brooke, home to Avalon," Gareth said, raising her thin hands to his lips and kissing her fingertips. "Ever since I got out of the service, I've worked at getting the gardens back in shape after all the months of neglect. It's going to be beautiful by the time we get there. And the house ... well, I want you to do whatever you wish inside. ... It will be yours now. ... You can bring your own things. ..."

"Dear Gareth," Brooke interrupted. "I have no things. Nothing is left of my beautiful screens or my porcelain or my Netsuke collection—all are gone, confiscated." A smile touched her mouth briefly. "I'm afraid I'm coming as your bride empty-handed."

"But not empty-hearted, my darling," Gareth replied, thinking how hard it must have been for Brooke to lose all her precious belongings.

"It doesn't matter. If there is one thing I've learned through all this, Gareth, it's that our material possessions are of little worth in the overall scheme of things. Only one thing is important: our relationship with God."

They were both silent a moment, letting the truth of her words seep in to them just as the beauty of the sunset filled them with awe and the majesty of its source. After a while Brooke asked, "Tell me again how it was your parents called your house Avalon."

"Actually, it was my Grandmother Blythe who named it. She

was totally enamored of the legend of King Arthur and the Knights of the Round Table. Avalon was part of that legend, the place to which Arthur returned and from which he would again rule. According to the Arthurian legends, it is a magical island hidden behind impenetrable mists. Unless you believe in its existence, the mists won't part." He paused. Brooke was listening attentively. "My father, Jeff Montrose, was named for the writer Geoffrey of Monmouth, who first chronicled the tales of Arthur.

"My parents inherited the estate, which actually is a small island, and perpetuated the myths of it being a special, secret place. They were completely in love with each other and the island, and they made it a magical one for us as children. My father needed the solitude to concentrate on his work, and my mother ensured that he had it. Meanwhile for us it became a closed but wonderful place, a kind of enchanted world-within-a-world." He smiled in tender remembrance. "Tennyson's *Idylls of the King* was the inspiration for many of my father's paintings, his style fashioned after the Pre-Raphaelite artists. My mother, Faith, was often his model." Gareth took Brooke's hand in his, covered it with his other hand, gave it a gentle squeeze.

"I remember the day you took me over there. I never dreamed then that one day I would live there."

"*I* knew," Gareth said. "But it was hard holding on to that dream."

Brooke gazed at him lovingly. To return to a dream required hope, a sense of childlike belief that dreams can come true, that prayers are answered. She thanked God that he had allowed her that dream, had given her the faith, the innocent hope she now saw as a miracle. That's what a miracle really is, after all: the parting of mists of doubt, unbelief, despair, to a fulfillment of love.

chapter
30

England

ALAIR HELD HER BREATH as she watched the men leave the train. So many things crowded into her mind as her eyes searched for him. She remembered the first time she had ever seen Luc Montrose, his confident walk, his cap at a jaunty angle, the ultimate cocky airman. And yet there had been a sensitive part of him, the sweet, poetic side of him that perhaps only she knew. The letters he had written from prison had revealed a man even deeper, more introspective, more spiritual, than she had glimpsed. The ordeal of being a prisoner of war would change anyone. He had written as if they might not ever see each other again, and yet in another few minutes Luc would step out of that train and—

Her first thought was how pale and thin he was. His uniform hung on his tall frame, the tunic collar loose. She was shocked to see he was leaning heavily on a cane as he emerged from the passenger car. Luc's leg had been broken in two places when he parachuted from his burning plane. She hadn't realized that he might be crippled. But perhaps it had not been set properly or had not healed well due to the horrible conditions in camp.

Luc did not see her right away, so she called out to him. She took a few steps, then halted. She couldn't seem to move any farther. Then she held out her arms, tears streaming down her face. His gait was awkward as he hobbled toward her. Dropping his cane, he went into her arms. She felt him sag against her, felt his shoulders shaking as they clung to each other wordlessly.

After a few minutes Alair gently disengaged herself, stooped and picked up his cane, handed it to him. "Come, darling, we're going home."

"Home?" he echoed, as if he'd never heard the word.

"Blanding Court, for now," she said, and holding his arm, she guided him toward the car parked at the curb, where Lady Blanding's chauffeur, Manning, waited, his own faded-blue eyes misty as the couple made their way toward him.

Luc stood looking down into the crib at his sleeping son. He put a gentle finger alongside the rosy cheek, touched the chubby hand, the golden curls. Alair came up beside him, slipped her hand through his arm. He turned and gazed down at her.

"Although I prayed for this day, I don't think I really believed it would ever happen," he said, smiling ironically. "That says a lot for my faith, doesn't it?"

"But darling, two years is a long time."

"It seemed an eternity. Sometimes I thought it would never end. To get through each day, I had to drag out what I could remember, what I had to come back to."

"The letters you wrote were full of faith, Luc. You made me believe. You kept me strong." Alair pressed his arm, leaned her head against his shoulder.

"We've lost so much time together," Luc sighed.

"We'll make up for it, darling," Alair said soothingly. "Mama has arranged with Jill Cameron for us to have Larkspur

Cottage. We're to take little Noel and go away, just the three of us, so we can get to know each other all over again and so you can get to know your little boy."

"I can't seem to think very far ahead, about the future. . . . I guess I'm so used to just thinking an hour at a time."

"It's all right, darling. Everything will be all right. We'll just take it one step at a time."

"I understand now why Aunt Kitty felt the way she did," Luc said. He might have said more, but he saw Alair's expression tighten and he realized she didn't want to talk about the war or what it had done to him, to both of them. Maybe he'd just have to keep his thoughts and feelings to himself for a while, until he was able to handle them. He'd have to keep them prisoner as he had been a prisoner. He had heard that unless you'd experienced it yourself, you couldn't understand. The attitude most of the POWs maintained—*had* to maintain, for their own protection, their own sanity—was to keep their emotions locked, never let their captors sense a vulnerability, a weakness. It was the only way to survive in a prison world. Luc was strong-willed. He had fought those black times when the despair and depression would overwhelm him. He'd learned how to close himself off from his own feelings. It had meant iron self-discipline. He'd lose track of time altogether. Days would go by and the black cloud would envelop him. Freedom came with a price. He would have to reverse what prison camp had taught him, not let Alair see that it was always hovering just behind him, over his shoulder, ready to pounce.

It was his problem, his battle to fight. He'd have to remember that. Alair had been through enough. He was determined not to burden her with his memories. He would eventually get over it, he prayed. In the meantime it was probably a good idea for them to go away together. He did feel somewhat like a biblical "stranger in a strange land." He had to learn to be normal again, had to build a life with Alair and their little son. Luc knew for sure that he wasn't ready to go back to America, to Virginia. He was still in shock after learning his father had been killed while he was in prison camp. Aunt Cara had closed Montclair afterward. Even so, Luc did not have the energy, the strength, the incentive, to go back to Mayfield and take over. He felt weary; he felt a hundred years old. Would he ever feel young again?

He didn't have to decide anything right away. Alair was already talking about packing, getting things together to leave for Jill's little cottage. There they would find each other again, find the love that had first brought them together, the love that had kept them together through the years of separation. At Larkspur Cottage, surely it would all come together for them again.

chapter
31

Blanding Court

ALAIR WANTED HER LIFE BACK, the lazy, golden days of that last summer when their love had been new—"love and the world well lost." She wanted Luc back, the way he was then, the Luc she had fallen in love with.

He sat on the terrace, his shadow falling on the sun-splashed stones. It seemed symbolic—Luc was a shadow of the man he had once been. . . .

The smile on his gaunt face with its hollowed cheekbones— the smile that never reached his haunted eyes. What was he looking at? What did he see? Lost comrades? The men with whom he had shared the brutal prison life? The ones who hadn't survived to come home—those who would never come home?

Alair's heart was wrenched. She felt a chill as the clouds passed over the sun, blocking it momentarily.

She chided herself, refusing to spoil what God had given her back. Hadn't she prayed night and day for Luc's return? Any way, any how, just so he would come back?

She remembered those long years of separation. It had always seemed to be winter. She knew that months had passed, that one by one the seasons had come, the spring turning into summer and then into fall . . . and yet to her, frozen in her longing, her grief, it had always seemed dreary, cold.

Then miraculously Luc had come back; against all odds he had been restored to her. Now it was up to her not to lose the future. God would bring it about, if only she would believe the promise, the one she had clung to through all those dark days: "I will never leave you nor forsake you." How she had held on to that, desperately, blindly. She must hold on to that now as well. God had brought her through the valley; she could depend on him to bring her through this too.

One day Luc would laugh again—how she missed that! He would look at his little son and see him, really see him. *What we have once loved we can never lose*—she'd read or heard that sometime, somewhere.

The sun came out from behind the clouds. Alair felt its warmth against her back as she went up the terrace steps toward Luc. She was carrying a box of plants, primroses to put in the flower box that edged the terrace. Planting was an act of faith, if anything was. Placing tiny seeds or starts in the earth and believing, hoping, that in time they would emerge in glorious blooms.

That was her belief, that Luc and she would again know the great intimacy, the closeness, they had once taken for granted. Even if her faith was just a tiny seed now, with God's grace it would strengthen and grow, just as would Luc's health—emotional, physical, spiritual. Alair knew in her heart of hearts that was so.

Luc's progress was slow and precarious. It was evident that he did not have the stamina, the energy, nor the desire to return to the States, take over Montclair. No one could expect that of him in his condition. That was quite clear to Cara when she came to see him at Larkspur Cottage.

Alair was very protective of him, and one evening after dinner, when Luc had excused himself, the two women talked long into the night.

"I don't know if Luc will ever regain his full health, Aunt Cara," Alair told her earnestly. "Quite frankly, I don't want him to tax himself in any way—after what he's been through these last three years. He must be given time to recover and get well. Here he will have every comfort, everything he needs to regain his strength. He's under the care of a very fine doctor, and mother and father want to give us a trip to Switzerland, to a wonderful resort there—for however long it takes for Luc to get back his health. I don't want him under any kind of pressure."

For all her gentleness, Alair's voice was very firm, her intention unmistakable.

Cara knew and understood what Alair was saying and what she had left unspoken as well. Kip was dead, Luc unable to take on the management of Montclair. Well, then, there was only one option left to her. Fraser. She would have to go to Scotland, talk to Phoebe and make her proposal.

Birchfields

Niki and Fraser walked along the path that led to the lake. "It seems strange here without Aunt Garnet," she said.

"She was a remarkable lady. I wish I'd had a chance to know her longer. I wish she'd known about us."

"I think she did. After she met you the first time, she said to Bryanne, 'Now there's a man strong enough for Niki.'" Niki laughed. "She was a romantic, you know. One of her favorite sayings was a French quotation, *'Dans la couer vous avais toujours vingt ans'*—'In your heart you are always twenty years old.'"

Fraser halted, pulled Niki close. She put her arms around him, lifted her face for his kiss. After a while they began walking again, swinging hands.

"Shouldn't we be making plans?" Fraser asked.

"What kind of plans?"

"Wedding plans, of course. I thought women were the ones who liked to talk about weddings."

"I hadn't really thought about it."

"Then it's time you did."

"Let's wait until Tante gets here," Niki suggested.

"In the meantime?"

"I was thinking I'd like to go to France. Pick up my search again . . ."

"I don't think this is a good time, do you? If things were bad when you were there before the war, they'd probably be chaotic now." He waited a minute to see how she'd respond, then said, "Darling, when it's the right time, I'll go with you."

"You will? But it's not important to you . . ."

"Niki, don't you know that anything that's important to you is important to me? From now on we're in this—whatever it is—together. That's the way I want it. Always."

1946

chapter

32

Scotland

CARA'S MEMORIES OF SCOTLAND were of her long-ago training as an ambulance driver in the Great War, the one they now called World War I. *Please, God,* she prayed, *may there never be a third.* She thought of Luc and Alair's baby, nearly the same age as Luc had been then. Cara controlled a shudder. Why, now that it was over, did she sympathize more with what Kitty's attitude had been all along? In her recent position with the Red Cross, Cara had dealt firsthand with the men flooding into veterans' hospitals. She had seen the hopelessness in their eyes, knowing they faced months, perhaps years, of multiple surgeries and rehabilitation therapy before they could resume their normal lives—if that would even be possible.

Of course, being with Luc had brought it all closer than before. She was almost thankful Kip had not lived to see Luc in his present condition. It would have broken his heart. *God has a purpose for everything, even the tragedies of our lives,* Cara thought, remembering how Owen had tried to tell her just that.

Now she had to face a new responsibility, and it weighed heavily upon her. Montclair. Who would take over what they had naturally expected would be Luc's inherited role? That's what she had to discuss with Phoebe.

Cara recalled the vibrant, pretty young governess Aunt Garnet had hired for the children during the family reunion at Birchfields in 1897, the year of Queen Victoria's Jubilee. She and Kitty had been six years old and full of mischief. Evalee had been there, too, and Phoebe had managed them all with patience, good humor, and tolerance. How surprised they had all been when Uncle Jonathan married her after Davida's death.

But she was exactly right for him. Down-to-earth, sensible, practical. Intelligent, understanding, sympathetic.

Cara was looking forward to renewing her acquaintance, especially now that they would have an even closer connection. She smiled, thinking of Niki's shining eyes and Fraser's glowing expression when they had met her in London and told her of their engagement.

Would Fraser be willing to come to Virginia and manage Montclair, the only home Niki had ever really known? How strong were his ties to his native land, his obligation to the family hotel business? Did Phoebe expect him to take over her job eventually? All this had to be found out, discussed, when Cara laid out her proposal to Phoebe. If it was turned down, then what? Cara did not even want to consider the alternative. Sell Montclair? The house where a Montrose had been master for over two hundred years?

The train rattled into the tiny station, and Cara left her compartment and stepped out onto the platform. The air was sharp, crisp, and damp. Cara turned up her coat collar and glanced around. She had not expected to be met. Trains were still running on irregular schedules as they slowly were converted from wartime troop transportation, and she had not been sure of her exact arrival time. Phoebe had told her the McPherson Arms was only a short walk and from the depot could be seen at the crest of the hill.

As Cara started up the winding street, she glanced about her with pleasure. Kingaren looked just the way a small Scottish town was supposed to—picturesque and charming. Stretching beyond it were rolling hills covered with heather and gorse, and the sweeping curves of distant mountains.

The McPherson Arms, which commanded the hillside it overlooked, was a timbered stucco-and-brick building. She entered the lobby and thought it more resembled a laird's country house than a hotel. Paneled walls were hung with pictures of men in full Highlander regalia. Comfortable chairs in faded plaid slipcovers were arranged in conversational groups before a wide stone fireplace, where a fire welcomed and warmed the weary traveler. As she stood on the threshold, she heard a soft voice with a musical lilt say her name. A tall woman came toward her, holding out both hands.

"Phoebe!" The two women embraced. "It's so good to see you."

"And you too. To think that we're going to be mother-in-law for each other's children!" Phoebe laughed. Its delightful sound took Cara back to her childhood, when Phoebe had joined in their play. "Come along. We'll have some tea straight away and a chance to talk."

Phoebe took Cara's arm and, passing the reception desk, said to the smiling young woman behind it, "This is my—what? My cousin? From America, Ellen. We're going back to my apartment. Will you have Annie bring us some tea, please?"

In Phoebe's apartment a small coal fire glowed, shining on the polished brass fender. "Do sit down and be comfortable, Cara. There's so much to talk about, so much I want to hear."

Cara hoped Phoebe would be open to her proposal and agree with her that Fraser was now the rightful heir to his father's estate.

Tea was brought in by a rosy-cheeked, cheerful maid. Cara, who had only had a hurried cup of tea and a stale bun at the London terminal tea shop, appreciated the hearty repast provided—freshly baked scones, shortbread, marmalade and lemon curd, and rich, strong tea. After the initial catching up was done, Cara brought up what she had traveled so far to discuss. She watched the other woman's face as she outlined her plan.

Phoebe had lost some of her youthful softness; her cheekbones were prominent and her eyes were thoughtful. She listened to all Cara had to say. Then she asked, "And have you discussed this with my son?"

"No, I wanted to talk with you first." Cara smiled. "Fraser was so besotted with Niki at the time, I didn't know whether he could discuss anything sensibly for a few weeks."

"I know. He is deeply in love with your daughter. I saw that when they were here."

"I believe he would do anything to make her happy. Montclair is Niki's home. She realizes that now more than ever. You know her background, of course?"

"Yes," Phoebe said, nodding. She was quiet for a long time. Then she spoke. "Like every mother whose son went to war, I suppose, I eagerly anticipated Fraser's safe return. Not that he ever wanted to take over the hotel. Oh, he worked here on school holidays and during the summer. But he's really a farmer. He talked often of having his own farm, raising sheep. So I should think the idea of having a place like Montclair would seem ideal to him." She paused and her eyes glowed momentarily with the brightness of tears. "And I think Jonathan would be very pleased."

chapter
33

Mayfield
June 1946

SOUTHERNERS ARE PARTICULARLY AWARE of the significance of heritage. So people in Mayfield buzzed with excitement at the announcement of Niki's engagement to Fraser Montrose. That the young couple would make their home at Montclair seemed singularly appropriate.

After all, the house had been built for Claire Fraser, the bride who had come to Virginia from Scotland to be its first mistress. Everything now seemed to fall perfectly in place with Niki and Fraser's marriage.

It was a storybook wedding. The Mayfield church was decorated with flowers from the gardens of many of the family's friends. Because there were still wartime shortages to be dealt with, the bride's dress was one borrowed from her Aunt Evalee. However, it was rumored to be a Chanel creation worn by Evalee at her wedding to a Russian prince. Niki's veil was an heirloom lace that had been worn by other Montrose brides. Her three cousins—Nora "Scotty" Cameron, Natasha Oblenskova, and Cara-Lyn Maynard, the senator's daughter—and the bridegroom's sister, Fiona Montrose, were her bridesmaids, gowned in pastel shades of organza.

In place of her late father, Captain Kip Montrose, the bride's uncle, Scott Cameron, would give the bride away.

In the vestibule Niki fidgeted while Aunt Jill adjusted her headdress of orange blossoms. "Hold still," Jill whispered.

"Sorry, I can't. I'm too excited," Niki apologized. Jill smiled. She had never seen a happier bride. How wonderful that everything had worked out so well.

Who would be the next bride? Jill wondered, casting a speculative glance at her own daughter. Scotty had had several wartime romances but nothing serious. Last night at the rehearsal dinner when they had cut the "prophecy cake," in which were baked tiny silver charms, Scotty had drawn the ring denoting the next engagement. *Well, we'll have to wait and see,* Jill thought. Scotty didn't give any inclination of settling down. Natasha had drawn the clover promising fortune. Maybe she would become a famous model, as her cousins were urging her to do, and make lots of money. Cara-Lyn had drawn the tiny wishing well, meaning she would get her secret wish, whatever that was. She was the serious, career-minded cousin, so who knew? The beautiful Scottish girl, Fiona, had drawn a star, and no one knew exactly what that predicted. It was lovely that she and Phoebe could come for the wedding.

Niki couldn't resist peeking through the doors into the sanctuary. She saw Fraser taking his place at the side of the altar. At her request he had worn his Highland regimental uniform, the kilt with the Graham tartan and all. The sun slanting in from the high arched windows burnished his reddish blond hair. *Oh, he's gorgeous,* Niki thought, and she sighed. *And he's mine! Almost, anyway.*

Just then someone thrust the bouquet of flowers into her hands. Their heavy fragrance rose and she took a deep breath. The first chords of Lohengrin's wedding march sounded.

"Time to go," Uncle Scott said, and Niki put her arm through his as someone pushed open the doors into the church.

Niki's heart fluttered. It was real. At last it was really happening. *Oh, I'm so glad we waited for this,* she thought. As they moved down the aisle, she felt the waves of love reaching out to her from people on either side. She felt the love surrounding her, wrapping her in its warmth and caring.

A heartfelt prayer rose up joyously in Niki. *Oh, thank you, God, for bringing me to this moment, to this country, to this family, to this man. In your love and wisdom, you brought me to this place so that I would be protected and cared for all the days of my life.*

With measured pace they reached the altar, and Uncle Scott placed Niki's hand in Fraser's extended one. Fraser's expression was serious until he looked down into Niki's radiant, upturned face, and then he broke into a wide smile.

The beautiful words that she'd listened to during the rehearsal she now spoke solemnly. She pledged her faithfulness, her devotion, her enduring love, to Fraser, whatever the future held. This time it was the real thing. The vows were forever. She thrilled at the sound of his soft burred voice as he made the same promises to her.

"You are now man and wife." This closed the formal ceremony. However, Niki and Fraser had decided to add something else. They moved up the altar steps together. Each took a taper and lit it from the two outside white candles in the branched silver candelabra.

The night before, Reverend Morrison had explained the significance of this part of the ceremony. The two end candles represented their separate lives up to this moment. Two distinct lights, capable of going separate ways. To bring happiness to their future home, these two lights must be merged into one light, as in the Lord's words: "A man shall leave his father and mother and be joined to his wife, and they will become one."

They had memorized what to say to each other.

"From this day forward, our thoughts shall be for each other rather than for our individual selves. Our plans shall be mutual. Our joys and our sorrows shall be shared alike."

Then together they used the flames of their individual candles to light the center one, saying in unison, "As we extinguish our separate candles thus, the center candle represents the sacred union of our lives. May this one light be a radiant testimony to our covenant to each other and our commitment to a Christian life together."

Niki could not remember ever being so filled with emotion, both happiness and a certain sadness. The leaving behind of the life she had known, especially in the past five years—her life of independence, adventure, self-reliance. From this day forward she would be living with entirely different purposes and goals. She was no longer hopelessly searching to belong somewhere, to someone. She had finally found a heart home.

Together they went back down the altar steps, stopping first at the Montrose pew to embrace Cara and Phoebe, then starting back down the aisle of the church. They halted here and there to shake hands, receive hugs and congratulations.

A photographer waited just outside in the vestibule, and flashbulbs popped, temporarily dazzling them as pictures were taken. Holding hands, they ran down the church steps. At the bottom Fraser swung Niki around into his arms and they kissed. A real kiss, not the brief, light one they had given each other at the close of the ceremony. When it ended they broke apart, laughing. Behind them they heard the footsteps and voices of the wedding guests following them out of the church and into the churchyard.

The Camerons had provided an old-fashioned horse-drawn carriage to take the newlywed couple to the reception. Those who understood the significance exchanged smiles and glances as the buggy disappeared down the country road. Again, as had happened in the many years past, a Montrose man was bringing home his bride to Montclair.

Look for these titles in Jane Peart's Brides of Montclair series at a Christian bookstore near you!

Valiant Bride
ISBN: 0-310-66951-0

A historical romance about a young woman's choice of duty over love.

Ransomed Bride
ISBN: 0-310-66961-8

In this sequel to *Valiant Bride,* Lorabeth Whitaker flees England and an undesirable marriage engagement.

Fortune's Bride
ISBN: 0-310-66971-5

Graham Montrose is widowed after only three months of marriage. He becomes the guardian of a 13-year-old girl, Avril. At her coming out party, he realizes his love for his ward.

Folly's Bride
ISBN: 0-310-66981-2

In a time of social unrest, slave rebellions, and growing political dissent, Sara, once impetuous and flirtatious, learns to overcome her pride as she comes under the influence of Clayborn Montrose, scion of the Montrose family and Master of Montclair.

Yankee Bride & Rebel Bride
ISBN: 0-310-66991-X

Against the turbulent backdrop of the Civil War, two beautiful women of strength and spirit struggle for the survival of their ideals, dreams, principles, and love. Their antagonism enacts the spiritual crisis of their time.

Destiny's Bride
ISBN: 0-310-67021-7

Destiny's Bride is the story of Druscilla Montrose.

Jubilee Bride
ISBN: 0-310-67121-3

In honor of Queen Victoria's Diamond Jubilee, the fiftieth year of her reign, Garnet invites both sides of her aristocratic Virginia family to England for a family reunion celebration.

Mirror Bride
ISBN: 0-310-67131-0

Mishap, romance, and mistaken identity are the ingredients for enlivening Virginia's prestigious Montrose family.

Hero's Bride
ISBN: 0-310-67141-8

The First World War is a time of testing and commitment as the eldest son goes to France to fight.

Daring Bride
ISBN: 0-310-20209-4

With the Depression clouding the present and World War II looming on the horizon, Aunt Garnet's ninetieth birthday is a reunion time for the Montrose and Cameron families.

Courageous Bride
ISBN: 0-310-20210-8

The First World War left Niki an orphan in France. Will World War II take away everything she holds dear—including Montclair, the only home she's ever known, and Fraser, the man she's grown to love?

ZondervanPublishingHouse
Grand Rapids, Michigan

A Division of HarperCollinsPublishers

Westward Dreams Romance Series from Jane Peart

Runaway Heart
ISBN: 0-310-41271-4

Heroine Holly Lambeth has escaped the humiliation of a broken engagement by visiting her cousin's family in Riverbend, Oregon. When her cousin proves less than hospitable, Holly is forced to find her own way in this very alien hostile culture.

Promise of the Valley
ISBN: 0-310-41281-1

When Southern-born Adelaide Pride follows her Yankee employer to California, she faces a private civil war and re-examines her values of love and honor.

Where Tomorrow Waits
ISBN: 0-310-41291-9

When calamity strikes, young Penny Sayres doubts her decision to trade the security of love for the adventure on the Oregon Trail.

A Distant Dawn
ISBN: 0-310-41301-X

When headstrong Sunny sets off to join the wagon train to California, she finds more adventure than she had planned.

The American Quilt Romance Series from Jane Peart

The Pattern
ISBN: 0-310-20166-7

Prior to the Civil War, well-to-do Johanna marries a doctor from
a poor family and moves to the harsh mountains of North Carolina.

The Pledge
ISBN: 0-310-20167-5

Johanna's daughter falls in love with a seminary student who is
cast out from the southern community when he chooses to fight for
the North.

The Promise
ISBN: 0-310-20168-3

Josie's daughter grows up in California and falls in love with a missionary who marries her and takes her to Hawaii, where adventures
await them.

ZondervanPublishingHouse
Grand Rapids, Michigan

A Division of HarperCollins*Publishers*

We want to hear from you. Please send your comments about this book to us in care of the address below. Thank you.

ZondervanPublishingHouse
Grand Rapids, Michigan 49530
http://www.zondervan.com